WAR AND PEACE

BOOK TEN : 1812

By Leo Tolstoy

War and Peace Book 10
by Leo Tolstoy

ISBN: 978-93-94973-97-8

Published by

DOUBLE 9 BOOKS

2/13-B, Ansari Road
Daryaganj, New Delhi - 110002
info@double9books.com
www.double9books.com
Tel. 011-40042856

Printed in India.

About the Author

L eo Tolstoy was a Russian creator known for his books War and Peace which is viewed as the best book of pragmatist fiction. Tolstoy is additionally viewed as world's best author by quite a few people. Additionally an ethical scholar and a social reformer, Tolstoy had extreme moralistic points of view. In later life, he turned into an intense Christian rebel and anarcho-conservative.

Leo Tolstoy Born in Yasnaya Polyana on September 9, 1828, He had a place with a notable honorable Russian family. He was the fourth among five offspring of Count Nikolai Ilyich Tolstoy and Countess Mariya Tolstaya, both of whom kicked the bucket passing on their youngsters to be raised by family members.

In 1844, Tolstoy was acknowledged into Kazan University. Incapable to graduate past the subsequent year, Tolstoy got back to Yasnava Polyana and afterward invested energy going among Moscow and St. Petersburg. With some functioning information on a few dialects, he turned into a multilingual. Yet again the recently observed youth pulled in Tolstoy towards drinking, visiting massage parlors and most betting which left him in weighty obligation and anguish however Tolstoy before long acknowledged he was carrying on with a brutish life and endeavored college tests with the expectation that he would acquire a situation with the public authority, yet finished yet up in Caucuses serving in the military continuing in the strides of his senior sibling.

In Year 1862, Leo Tolstoy wedded Sophia Andreevna Behrs, generally called Sonya, who was 16 years more youthful than him. The couple had thirteen youngsters, of which, five passed on at an early age. Sonya went about as Tolstoy's secretary, editor and monetary chief while he made two out of his most prominent works. Their initial wedded life was loaded up with happiness.

He started composing his show-stopper, War and Peace in 1862. The six volumes of the work were distributed somewhere in the range of 1863 and 1869. With 580 characters got from history and others made by Tolstoy, this extraordinary novel takes on investigating the hypothesis of history and the irrelevance of noted figures like Alexander and Napoleon. Anna Karenina, Tolstoy's next epic was begun in 1873 and distributed totally in 1878.

Contents

BOOK TEN : 1812

CHAPTER I

Napoleon began the war with Russia because he could not resist going to Dresden, could not help having his head turned by the homage he received, could not help donning a Polish uniform and yielding to the stimulating influence of a June morning, and could not refrain from bursts of anger in the presence of Kurákin and then of Balashëv.

Alexander refused negotiations because he felt himself to be personally insulted. Barclay de Tolly tried to command the army in the best way, because he wished to fulfill his duty and earn fame as a great commander. Rostóv charged the French because he could not restrain his wish for a gallop across a level field; and in the same way the innumerable people who took part in the war acted in accord with their personal characteristics, habits, circumstances, and aims. They were moved by fear or vanity, rejoiced or were indignant, reasoned, imagining that they knew what they were doing and did it of their own free will, but they all were involuntary tools of history, carrying on a work concealed from them but comprehensible to us. Such is the inevitable fate of men of action, and the higher they stand in the social hierarchy the less are they free.

The actors of 1812 have long since left the stage, their personal interests have vanished leaving no trace, and nothing remains of that time but its historic results.

Providence compelled all these men, striving to attain personal aims, to further the accomplishment of a stupendous result no one of them at all expected—neither Napoleon, nor Alexander, nor still less any of those who did the actual fighting.

The cause of the destruction of the French army in 1812 is clear to us now. No one will deny that that cause was, on the one hand, its advance into the heart of Russia late in the season without any preparation for a winter campaign and, on the other, the character given to the war by the burning of Russian towns and the hatred of the foe this aroused among the Russian people. But no one at the time foresaw (what now seems so evident) that this was the only way an army of eight hundred thousand men—the best in the world and led by the best general—could be destroyed in conflict with a raw army of half its numerical strength, and led by inexperienced commanders as the Russian army was. *Not only did no one see this*, but *on the Russian side* every effort was made to hinder the only thing that could save Russia, while *on the French side*, despite Napoleon's experience and so-called military genius, every effort was directed to pushing on to Moscow at the end of the summer, that is, to doing the very thing that was bound to lead to destruction.

In historical works on the year 1812 French writers are very fond of saying that Napoleon felt the danger of extending his line, that he sought a battle and that his marshals advised him to stop at Smolénsk, and of making similar statements to show that the danger of the campaign was even then understood. Russian authors are still fonder of telling us that from the commencement of the campaign a Scythian war plan was adopted to lure Napoleon into the depths of Russia, and this plan some of them attribute to Pfuel, others to a certain Frenchman, others to Toll, and others again to Alexander himself—pointing to notes, projects, and letters which contain hints of such a line of action. But all these hints at what happened, both from the French side and the Russian, are advanced only because they fit in with the event. Had that event not occurred these hints would have been forgotten, as we have forgotten the thousands and millions of hints and expectations to the contrary which were current then but have now been forgotten because the event falsified them. There are always so many conjectures as to the issue of any event that however it may end there will always be people to say: "I said then that it would be so," quite forgetting that amid their innumerable conjectures many were to quite the contrary effect.

Conjectures as to Napoleon's awareness of the danger of extending his line, and (on the Russian side) as to luring the enemy into the depths of Russia, are evidently of that kind, and only by much straining can historians attribute such conceptions to Napoleon and his marshals, or such plans to the Russian commanders. All the facts are in flat contradiction to such conjectures. During the whole period of the war not only was there no wish on the Russian side to draw the French into the heart of the country, but from their first entry into Russia everything was done to stop them. And not only was Napoleon not afraid to extend his line, but he welcomed every step forward as a triumph and did not seek battle as eagerly as in former campaigns, but very lazily.

At the very beginning of the war our armies were divided, and our sole aim was to unite them, though uniting the armies was no advantage if we meant to retire and lure the enemy into the depths of the country. Our Emperor joined the army to encourage it to defend every inch of Russian soil and not to retreat. The enormous Drissa camp was formed on Pfuel's plan, and there was no intention of retiring farther. The Emperor reproached the commanders in chief for every step they retired. He could not bear the idea of letting the enemy even reach Smolénsk, still less could he contemplate the burning of Moscow, and when our armies did unite he was displeased that Smolénsk was abandoned and burned without a general engagement having been fought under its walls.

So thought the Emperor, and the Russian commanders and people were still more provoked at the thought that our forces were retreating into the depths of the country.

Napoleon having cut our armies apart advanced far into the country and missed several chances of forcing an engagement. In August he was at Smolénsk and thought only of how to advance farther, though as we now see that advance was evidently ruinous to him.

The facts clearly show that Napoleon did not foresee the danger of the advance on Moscow, nor did Alexander and the Russian commanders then think of luring Napoleon on, but quite the contrary. The luring of Napoleon into the depths of the country was not the result of any plan, for no one believed it to be possible; it resulted from a most complex interplay of intrigues, aims, and wishes among those who took part in the war and had no perception whatever of the inevitable, or of the one way of saving Russia. Everything came about fortuitously. The armies were divided at the commencement of the campaign. We tried to unite them, with the evident intention of giving battle and checking the enemy's advance, and by this effort to unite them while avoiding battle with a much stronger enemy, and necessarily withdrawing the armies at an acute angle—we led the French on to Smolénsk. But we withdrew at an acute angle not only because the French advanced between our two armies; the angle became still more acute and we withdrew still farther, because Barclay de Tolly was an unpopular foreigner disliked by Bagratión (who would come under his command), and Bagratión—being in command of the second army—tried to postpone joining up and coming under Barclay's command as long as he could. Bagratión was slow in effecting the junction—though that was the chief aim of all at headquarters—because, as he alleged, he exposed his army to danger on this march, and it was best for him to retire more to the left and more to the south, worrying the enemy from flank and rear and securing from the Ukraine recruits for his army; and it looks as if he planned this in order not to come under the command of the detested foreigner Barclay, whose rank was inferior to his own.

The Emperor was with the army to encourage it, but his presence and ignorance of what steps to take, and the enormous number of advisers and plans, destroyed the first army's energy and it retired.

The intention was to make a stand at the Drissa camp, but Paulucci, aiming at becoming commander in chief, unexpectedly employed his energy to influence Alexander, and Pfuel's whole plan was abandoned and the command entrusted to Barclay. But as Barclay did not inspire confidence his power was limited. The armies were divided, there was no unity of command, and Barclay was unpopular; but from this confusion, division, and the unpopularity of the foreign commander in chief, there resulted on the one hand indecision and the avoidance of a battle (which we could not have refrained from had the armies been united and had someone else, instead of Barclay, been in command) and on the other an ever-increasing indignation against the foreigners and an increase in patriotic zeal.

At last the Emperor left the army, and as the most convenient and indeed the only pretext for his departure it was decided that it was necessary for him to inspire the people in the capitals and arouse the nation in general to a patriotic war. And by this visit of the Emperor to Moscow the strength of the Russian army was trebled.

He left in order not to obstruct the commander in chief's undivided control of the army, and hoping that more decisive action would then be taken, but the command of the armies became still more confused and enfeebled. Bennigsen, the Tsarévich, and a swarm of adjutants general remained with the army to keep the commander in chief under observation and arouse his energy, and Barclay, feeling less free than ever under the observation of all these "eyes of the Emperor," became still more cautious of undertaking any decisive action and avoided giving battle.

Barclay stood for caution. The Tsarévich hinted at treachery and demanded a general engagement. Lubomírski, Bronnítski, Wlocki, and the others of that group stirred up so much trouble that Barclay, under pretext of sending papers to the Emperor, dispatched these Polish adjutants general to Petersburg and plunged into an open struggle with Bennigsen and the Tsarévich.

At Smolénsk the armies at last reunited, much as Bagratión disliked it.

Bagratión drove up in a carriage to the house occupied by Barclay. Barclay donned his sash and came out to meet and report to his senior officer Bagratión.

Despite his seniority in rank Bagratión, in this contest of magnanimity, took his orders from Barclay, but, having submitted, agreed with him less than ever. By the Emperor's orders Bagratión reported direct to him. He wrote to Arakchéev, the Emperor's confidant: "It must be as my sovereign pleases, but I cannot work with the *Minister* (meaning Barclay). For God's sake send me somewhere else if only in command of a regiment. I cannot stand it here. Headquarters are so full of Germans that a Russian cannot exist and there is no sense in anything. I thought I was really serving my sovereign and the Fatherland, but it turns out that I am serving Barclay. I confess I do not want to."

The swarm of Bronnítskis and Wintzingerodes and their like still further embittered the relations between the commanders in chief, and even less unity resulted. Preparations were made to fight the French before Smolénsk. A general was sent to survey the position. This general, hating Barclay, rode to visit a friend of his own, a corps commander, and, having spent the day with him, returned to Barclay and condemned, as unsuitable from every point of view, the battleground he had not seen.

While disputes and intrigues were going on about the future field of battle, and while we were looking for the French—having lost touch with them—the French stumbled upon Nevérovski's division and reached the walls of Smolénsk.

It was necessary to fight an unexpected battle at Smolénsk to save our lines of communication. The battle was fought and thousands were killed on both sides.

Smolénsk was abandoned contrary to the wishes of the Emperor and of the whole people. But Smolénsk was burned by its own inhabitants who had been misled by their governor. And these ruined inhabitants, setting an example to other Russians, went to Moscow thinking only of their own losses but kindling hatred of the foe. Napoleon advanced farther and we retired, thus arriving at the very result which caused his destruction.

CHAPTER II

The day after his son had left, Prince Nicholas sent for Princess Mary to come to his study.

"Well? Are you satisfied now?" said he. "You've made me quarrel with my son! Satisfied, are you? That's all you wanted! Satisfied?... It hurts me, it hurts. I'm old and weak and this is what you wanted. Well then, gloat over it! Gloat over it!"

After that Princess Mary did not see her father for a whole week. He was ill and did not leave his study.

Princess Mary noticed to her surprise that during this illness the old prince not only excluded her from his room, but did not admit Mademoiselle Bourienne either. Tíkhon alone attended him.

At the end of the week the prince reappeared and resumed his former way of life, devoting himself with special activity to building operations and the arrangement of the gardens and completely breaking off his relations with Mademoiselle Bourienne. His looks and cold tone to his daughter seemed to say: "There, you see? You plotted against me, you lied to Prince Andrew about my relations with that Frenchwoman and made me quarrel with him, but you see I need neither her nor you!"

Princess Mary spent half of every day with little Nicholas, watching his lessons, teaching him Russian and music herself, and talking to Dessalles; the rest of the day she spent over her books, with her old nurse, or with "God's folk" who sometimes came by the back door to see her.

Of the war Princess Mary thought as women do think about wars. She feared for her brother who was in it, was horrified by and amazed at the strange cruelty that impels men to kill one another, but she did not understand the significance of this war, which seemed to her like all previous wars. She did not realize the significance of this war, though Dessalles with whom she constantly conversed was passionately interested in its progress and tried to explain his own conception of it to her, and though the "God's folk" who came to see her reported, in their own way, the rumors current among the people of an invasion by Antichrist, and though Julie (now Princess Drubetskáya), who had resumed correspondence with her, wrote patriotic letters from Moscow.

"I write you in Russian, my good friend," wrote Julie in her Frenchified Russian, "because I have a detestation for all the French, and the same for their language which I cannot support to hear spoken.... We in Moscow are elated by enthusiasm for our adored Emperor.

"My poor husband is enduring pains and hunger in Jewish taverns, but the news which I have inspires me yet more.

"You heard probably of the heroic exploit of Raévski, embracing his two sons and saying: 'I will perish with them but we will not be shaken!' And truly though the enemy was twice stronger than we, we were unshakable. We pass the time as we can, but in war as in war! The princesses Aline and Sophie sit whole days with me, and we, unhappy widows of live men, make beautiful conversations over our *charpie*, only you, my friend, are missing..." and so on.

The chief reason Princess Mary did not realize the full significance of this war was that the old prince never spoke of it, did not recognize it, and laughed at Dessalles when he mentioned it at dinner. The prince's tone was so calm and confident that Princess Mary unhesitatingly believed him.

All that July the old prince was exceedingly active and even animated. He planned another garden and began a new building for the domestic serfs. The only thing that made Princess Mary anxious about him was that he slept very little and, instead of sleeping in his study as usual, changed his sleeping place every day. One day he would order his camp bed to be set up in the glass gallery, another day he remained on the couch or on the lounge chair in the drawing room and dozed there without undressing, while—instead of Mademoiselle Bourienne—a serf boy read to him. Then again he would spend a night in the dining room.

On August 1, a second letter was received from Prince Andrew. In his first letter which came soon after he had left home, Prince Andrew had dutifully asked his father's forgiveness for what he had allowed himself to say and begged to be restored to his favor. To this letter the old prince had replied affectionately, and from that time had kept the Frenchwoman at a distance. Prince Andrew's second letter, written near Vítebsk after the French had occupied that town, gave a brief account of the whole campaign, enclosed for them a plan he had drawn and forecasts as to the further progress of the war. In this letter Prince Andrew pointed out to his father the danger of staying at Bald Hills, so near the theater of war and on the army's direct line of march, and advised him to move to Moscow.

At dinner that day, on Dessalles' mentioning that the French were said to have already entered Vítebsk, the old prince remembered his son's letter.

"There was a letter from Prince Andrew today," he said to Princess Mary—"Haven't you read it?"

"No, Father," she replied in a frightened voice.

She could not have read the letter as she did not even know it had arrived.

"He writes about this war," said the prince, with the ironic smile that had become habitual to him in speaking of the present war.

"That must be very interesting," said Dessalles. "Prince Andrew is in a position to know..."

"Oh, very interesting!" said Mademoiselle Bourienne.

"Go and get it for me," said the old prince to Mademoiselle Bourienne. "You know—under the paperweight on the little table."

Mademoiselle Bourienne jumped up eagerly.

"No, don't!" he exclaimed with a frown. "You go, Michael Ivánovich."

Michael Ivánovich rose and went to the study. But as soon as he had left the room the old prince, looking uneasily round, threw down his napkin and went himself.

"They can't do anything... always make some muddle," he muttered.

While he was away Princess Mary, Dessalles, Mademoiselle Bourienne, and even little Nicholas exchanged looks in silence. The old prince returned with quick steps, accompanied by Michael Ivánovich, bringing the letter and a plan. These he put down beside him—not letting anyone read them at dinner.

On moving to the drawing room he handed the letter to Princess Mary and, spreading out before him the plan of the new building and fixing his eyes upon it, told her to read the letter aloud. When she had done so Princess Mary looked inquiringly at her father. He was examining the plan, evidently engrossed in his own ideas.

"What do you think of it, Prince?" Dessalles ventured to ask.

"I? I?..." said the prince as if unpleasantly awakened, and not taking his eyes from the plan of the building.

"Very possibly the theater of war will move so near to us that..."

"Ha haha! The theater of war!" said the prince. "I have said and still say that the theater of war is Poland and the enemy will never get beyond the Niemen."

Dessalles looked in amazement at the prince, who was talking of the Niemen when the enemy was already at the Dnieper, but Princess Mary, forgetting the geographical position of the Niemen, thought that what her father was saying was correct.

"When the snow melts they'll sink in the Polish swamps. Only they could fail to see it," the prince continued, evidently thinking of the campaign of 1807 which seemed to him so recent. "Bennigsen should have advanced into Prussia sooner, then things would have taken a different turn..."

"But, Prince," Dessalles began timidly, "the letter mentions Vítebsk...."

"Ah, the letter? Yes..." replied the prince peevishly. "Yes... yes..." His face suddenly took on a morose expression. He paused. "Yes, he writes that the French were beaten at... at... what river is it?"

Dessalles dropped his eyes.

"The prince says nothing about that," he remarked gently.

"Doesn't he? But I didn't invent it myself."

No one spoke for a long time.

"Yes... yes... Well, Michael Ivánovich," he suddenly went on, raising his head and pointing to the plan of the building, "tell me how you mean to alter it...."

Michael Ivánovich went up to the plan, and the prince after speaking to him about the building looked angrily at Princess Mary and Dessalles and went to his own room.

Princess Mary saw Dessalles' embarrassed and astonished look fixed on her father, noticed his silence, and was struck by the fact that her father had forgotten his son's letter on the drawing room table; but she was not only afraid to speak of it and ask Dessalles the reason of his confusion and silence, but was afraid even to think about it.

In the evening Michael Ivánovich, sent by the prince, came to Princess Mary for Prince Andrew's letter which had been forgotten in the drawing room. She gave it to him and, unpleasant as it was to her to do so, ventured to ask him what her father was doing.

"Always busy," replied Michael Ivánovich with a respectfully ironic smile which caused Princess Mary to turn pale. "He's worrying very much about the new building. He has been reading a little, but now"—Michael Ivánovich went on, lowering his voice—"now he's at his desk, busy with his will, I expect." (One of the prince's favorite occupations of late had been the preparation of some papers he meant to leave at his death and which he called his "will.")

"And Alpátych is being sent to Smolénsk?" asked Princess Mary.

"Oh, yes, he has been waiting to start for some time."

CHAPTER III

When Michael Ivánovich returned to the study with the letter, the old prince, with spectacles on and a shade over his eyes, was sitting at his open bureau with screened candles, holding a paper in his outstretched hand, and in a somewhat dramatic attitude was reading his manuscript—his "Remarks" as he termed it—which was to be transmitted to the Emperor after his death.

When Michael Ivánovich went in there were tears in the prince's eyes evoked by the memory of the time when the paper he was now reading had been written. He took the letter from Michael Ivánovich's hand, put it in his pocket, folded up his papers, and called in Alpátych who had long been waiting.

The prince had a list of things to be bought in Smolénsk and, walking up and down the room past Alpátych who stood by the door, he gave his instructions.

"First, notepaper—do you hear? Eight quires, like this sample, gilt-edged... it must be exactly like the sample. Varnish, sealing wax, as in Michael Ivánovich's list."

He paced up and down for a while and glanced at his notes.

"Then hand to the governor in person a letter about the deed."

Next, bolts for the doors of the new building were wanted and had to be of a special shape the prince had himself designed, and a leather case had to be ordered to keep the "will" in.

The instructions to Alpátych took over two hours and still the prince did not let him go. He sat down, sank into thought, closed his eyes, and dozed off. Alpátych made a slight movement.

"Well, go, go! If anything more is wanted I'll send after you."

Alpátych went out. The prince again went to his bureau, glanced into it, fingered his papers, closed the bureau again, and sat down at the table to write to the governor.

It was already late when he rose after sealing the letter. He wished to sleep, but he knew he would not be able to and that most depressing thoughts came to him in bed. So he called Tíkhon and went through the rooms with him to show him where to set up the bed for that night.

He went about looking at every corner. Every place seemed unsatisfactory, but worst of all was his customary couch in the study. That couch was dreadful to him, probably because of the oppressive thoughts he had had when lying there. It was unsatisfactory everywhere, but the corner behind the piano in the sitting room was better than other places: he had never slept there yet.

With the help of a footman Tíkhon brought in the bedstead and began putting it up.

"That's not right! That's not right!" cried the prince, and himself pushed it a few inches from the corner and then closer in again.

"Well, at last I've finished, now I'll rest," thought the prince, and let Tíkhon undress him.

Frowning with vexation at the effort necessary to divest himself of his coat and trousers, the prince undressed, sat down heavily on the bed, and appeared to be meditating as he looked contemptuously at his withered yellow legs. He was not meditating, but only deferring the moment of making the effort to lift those legs up and turn over on the bed. "Ugh, how hard it is! Oh, that this toil might end and *you* would release me!" thought he. Pressing his lips together he made that effort for the twenty-thousandth time and lay down. But hardly had he done so before he felt the bed rocking backwards and forwards beneath him as if it were breathing heavily and jolting. This happened to him almost every night. He opened his eyes as they were closing.

"No peace, damn them!" he muttered, angry he knew not with whom. "Ah yes, there was something else important, very important, that I was keeping till I should be in bed. The bolts? No, I told him about them. No, it was something, something in the drawing room.

Princess Mary talked some nonsense. Dessalles, that fool, said something. Something in my pocket—can't remember...."

"Tíkhon, what did we talk about at dinner?"

"About Prince Michael..."

"Be quiet, quiet!" The prince slapped his hand on the table. "Yes, I know, Prince Andrew's letter! Princess Mary read it. Dessalles said something about Vítebsk. Now I'll read it."

He had the letter taken from his pocket and the table—on which stood a glass of lemonade and a spiral wax candle—moved close to the bed, and putting on his spectacles he began reading. Only now in the stillness of the night, reading it by the faint light under the green shade, did he grasp its meaning for a moment.

"The French at Vítebsk, in four days' march they may be at Smolénsk; perhaps are already there! Tíkhon!" Tíkhon jumped up. "No, no, I don't want anything!" he shouted.

He put the letter under the candlestick and closed his eyes. And there rose before him the Danube at bright noonday: reeds, the Russian camp, and himself a young general without a wrinkle on his ruddy face, vigorous and alert, entering Potëmkin's gaily colored tent, and a burning sense of jealousy of "the favorite" agitated him now as strongly as it had done then. He recalled all the words spoken at that first meeting with Potëmkin. And he saw before him a plump, rather sallow-faced, short, stout woman, the Empress Mother, with her smile and her words at her first gracious reception of him, and then that same face on the catafalque, and the encounter he had with Zúbov over her coffin about his right to kiss her hand.

"Oh, quicker, quicker! To get back to that time and have done with all the present! Quicker, quicker—and that they should leave me in peace!"

CHAPTER IV

B ald Hills, Prince Nicholas Bolkónski's estate, lay forty miles east from Smolénsk and two miles from the main road to Moscow.

The same evening that the prince gave his instructions to Alpátych, Dessalles, having asked to see Princess Mary, told her that, as the prince was not very well and was taking no steps to secure his safety, though from Prince Andrew's letter it was evident that to remain at Bald Hills might be dangerous, he respectfully advised her to send a letter by Alpátych to the Provincial Governor at Smolénsk, asking him to let her know the state of affairs and the extent of the danger to which Bald Hills was exposed. Dessalles wrote this letter to the Governor for Princess Mary, she signed it, and it was given to Alpátych with instructions to hand it to the Governor and to come back as quickly as possible if there was danger.

Having received all his orders Alpátych, wearing a white beaver hat—a present from the prince—and carrying a stick as the prince did, went out accompanied by his family. Three well-fed roans stood ready harnessed to a small conveyance with a leather hood.

The larger bell was muffled and the little bells on the harness stuffed with paper. The prince allowed no one at Bald Hills to drive with ringing bells; but on a long journey Alpátych liked to have them. His satellites—the senior clerk, a countinghouse clerk, a scullery maid, a cook, two old women, a little pageboy, the coachman, and various domestic serfs—were seeing him off.

His daughter placed chintz-covered down cushions for him to sit on and behind his back. His old sister-in-law popped in a small bundle, and one of the coachmen helped him into the vehicle.

"There! There! Women's fuss! Women, women!" said Alpátych, puffing and speaking rapidly just as the prince did, and he climbed into the trap.

After giving the clerk orders about the work to be done, Alpátych, not trying to imitate the prince now, lifted the hat from his bald head and crossed himself three times.

"If there is anything... come back, YákovAlpátych! For Christ's sake think of us!" cried his wife, referring to the rumors of war and the enemy.

"Women, women! Women's fuss!" muttered Alpátych to himself and started on his journey, looking round at the fields of yellow rye and the still-green, thickly growing oats, and at other quite black fields just being plowed a second time.

As he went along he looked with pleasure at the year's splendid crop of corn, scrutinized the strips of ryefield which here and there were already being reaped, made his calculations as to the sowing and the harvest, and asked himself whether he had not forgotten any of the prince's orders.

Having baited the horses twice on the way, he arrived at the town toward evening on the fourth of August.

Alpátych kept meeting and overtaking baggage trains and troops on the road. As he approached Smolénsk he heard the sounds of distant firing, but these did not impress him. What struck him most was the sight of a splendid field of oats in which a camp had been pitched and which was being mown down by the soldiers, evidently for fodder. This fact impressed Alpátych, but in thinking about his own business he soon forgot it.

All the interests of his life for more than thirty years had been bounded by the will of the prince, and he never went beyond that limit. Everything not connected with the execution of the prince's orders did not interest and did not even exist for Alpátych.

On reaching Smolénsk on the evening of the fourth of August he put up in the Gáchina suburb across the Dnieper, at the inn kept by Ferapóntov, where he had been in the habit of putting up for the last thirty years. Some thirty years ago Ferapóntov, by Alpátych's advice, had bought a wood from the prince, had begun to trade, and now had a house, an inn, and a corn dealer's shop in that province. He was a stout, dark, red-faced peasant in the forties, with thick lips, a broad knob of a nose, similar knobs over his black frowning brows, and a round belly.

Wearing a waistcoat over his cotton shirt, Ferapóntov was standing before his shop which opened onto the street. On seeing Alpátych he went up to him.

"You're welcome, YákovAlpátych. Folks are leaving the town, but you have come to it," said he.

"Why are they leaving the town?" asked Alpátych.

"That's what I say. Folks are foolish! Always afraid of the French."

"Women's fuss, women's fuss!" said Alpátych.

"Just what I think, YákovAlpátych. What I say is: orders have been given not to let them in, so that must be right. And the peasants are asking three rubles for carting—it isn't Christian!"

YákovAlpátych heard without heeding. He asked for a samovar and for hay for his horses, and when he had had his tea he went to bed.

All night long troops were moving past the inn. Next morning Alpátych donned a jacket he wore only in town and went out on business. It was a sunny morning and by eight o'clock it was already hot. "A good day for harvesting," thought Alpátych.

From beyond the town firing had been heard since early morning. At eight o'clock the booming of cannon was added to the sound of musketry. Many people were hurrying through the streets and there were many soldiers, but cabs were still driving about, tradesmen stood at their shops, and service was being held in the churches as usual. Alpátych went to the shops, to government offices, to the post office, and to the Governor's. In the offices and shops and at the post office everyone was talking about the army and about the enemy who was already attacking the town, everybody was asking what should be done, and all were trying to calm one another.

In front of the Governor's house Alpátych found a large number of people, Cossacks, and a traveling carriage of the Governor's. At the porch he met two of the landed gentry, one of whom he knew. This man, an ex-captain of police, was saying angrily:

"It's no joke, you know! It's all very well if you're single. 'One man though undone is but one,' as the proverb says, but with thirteen in your family and all the property... They've brought us to utter ruin! What sort of governors are they to do that? They ought to be hanged—the brigands!..."

"Oh come, that's enough!" said the other.

"What do I care? Let him hear! We're not dogs," said the ex-captain of police, and looking round he noticed Alpátych.

"Oh, YákovAlpátych! What have you come for?"

"To see the Governor by his excellency's order," answered Alpátych, lifting his head and proudly thrusting his hand into the bosom of his coat as he always did when he mentioned the prince.... "He has ordered me to inquire into the position of affairs," he added.

"Yes, go and find out!" shouted the angry gentleman. "They've brought things to such a pass that there are no carts or anything!... There it is again, do you hear?" said he, pointing in the direction whence came the sounds of firing.

"They've brought us all to ruin... the brigands!" he repeated, and descended the porch steps.

Alpátych swayed his head and went upstairs. In the waiting room were tradesmen, women, and officials, looking silently at one another. The door of the Governor's room opened and they all rose and moved forward. An official ran out, said some words to a merchant, called a stout official with a cross hanging on his neck to follow him, and vanished again, evidently wishing to avoid the inquiring looks and questions addressed to him. Alpátych moved forward and next time the official came out addressed him, one hand placed in the breast of his buttoned coat, and handed him two letters.

"To his Honor Baron Asch, from General-in-Chief Prince Bolkónski," he announced with such solemnity and significance that the official turned to him and took the letters.

A few minutes later the Governor received Alpátych and hurriedly said to him:

"Inform the prince and princess that I knew nothing: I acted on the highest instructions—here..." and he handed a paper to Alpátych. "Still, as the prince is unwell my advice is that they should go to Moscow. I am just starting myself. Inform them..."

But the Governor did not finish: a dusty perspiring officer ran into the room and began to say something in French. The Governor's face expressed terror.

"Go," he said, nodding his head to Alpátych, and began questioning the officer.

Eager, frightened, helpless glances were turned on Alpátych when he came out of the Governor's room. Involuntarily listening now to the firing, which had drawn nearer and was increasing in strength, Alpátych hurried to his inn. The paper handed to him by the Governor said this:

"I assure you that the town of Smolénsk is not in the slightest danger as yet and it is unlikely that it will be threatened with any. I from the one side and Prince Bagratión from the other are marching to unite our forces before Smolénsk, which junction will be effected on the 22nd instant, and both armies with their united forces will defend our compatriots of the province entrusted to your care till our efforts shall have beaten back the enemies of our Fatherland, or till the last warrior in our valiant ranks has perished. From this you will see that you have a perfect right to reassure the inhabitants of Smolénsk, for those defended by two such brave armies may feel assured of victory." (Instructions from Barclay de Tolly to Baron Asch, the civil governor of Smolénsk, 1812.)

People were anxiously roaming about the streets.

Carts piled high with household utensils, chairs, and cupboards kept emerging from the gates of the yards and moving along the streets. Loaded carts stood at the house next to Ferapóntov's and women were wailing and lamenting as they said good-by. A small watchdog ran round barking in front of the harnessed horses.

Alpátych entered the innyard at a quicker pace than usual and went straight to the shed where his horses and trap were. The coachman was asleep. He woke him up, told him to harness, and went into the passage. From the host's room came the sounds of a child crying, the despairing sobs of a woman, and the hoarse angry shouting of Ferapóntov. The cook began running hither and thither in the passage like a frightened hen, just as Alpátych entered.

"He's done her to death. Killed the mistress!... Beat her... dragged her about so!..."

"What for?" asked Alpátych.

"She kept begging to go away. She's a woman! 'Take me away,' says she, 'don't let me perish with my little children! Folks,' she says, 'are all gone, so why,' she says, 'don't we go?' And he began beating and pulling her about so!"

At these words Alpátych nodded as if in approval, and not wishing to hear more went to the door of the room opposite the innkeeper's, where he had left his purchases.

"You brute, you murderer!" screamed a thin, pale woman who, with a baby in her arms and her kerchief torn from her head, burst through the door at that moment and down the steps into the yard.

Ferapóntov came out after her, but on seeing Alpátych adjusted his waistcoat, smoothed his hair, yawned, and followed Alpátych into the opposite room.

"Going already?" said he.

Alpátych, without answering or looking at his host, sorted his packages and asked how much he owed.

"We'll reckon up! Well, have you been to the Governor's?" asked Ferapóntov. "What has been decided?"

Alpátych replied that the Governor had not told him anything definite.

"With our business, how can we get away?" said Ferapóntov. "We'd have to pay seven rubles a cartload to Dorogobúzh and I tell them they're not Christians to ask it! Selivánov, now, did a good stroke last Thursday—sold flour to the army at nine rubles a sack. Will you have some tea?" he added.

While the horses were being harnessed Alpátych and Ferapóntov over their tea talked of the price of corn, the crops, and the good weather for harvesting.

"Well, it seems to be getting quieter," remarked Ferapóntov, finishing his third cup of tea and getting up. "Ours must have got the best of it. The orders were not to let them in. So we're in force, it seems.... They say the other day Matthew IványchPlátov drove them into the river Márina and drowned some eighteen thousand in one day."

Alpátych collected his parcels, handed them to the coachman who had come in, and settled up with the innkeeper. The noise of wheels, hoofs, and bells was heard from the gateway as a little trap passed out.

It was by now late in the afternoon. Half the street was in shadow, the other half brightly lit by the sun. Alpátych looked out of the window and went to the door. Suddenly the strange sound of a far-off whistling and thud was heard, followed by a boom of cannon blending into a dull roar that set the windows rattling.

He went out into the street: two men were running past toward the bridge. From different sides came whistling sounds and the thud of cannon balls and bursting shells falling on the town. But these sounds were hardly heard in comparison with the noise of the firing outside the town and attracted little attention from the inhabitants. The town was being bombarded by a hundred and thirty guns which Napoleon had ordered up after four o'clock. The people did not at once realize the meaning of this bombardment.

At first the noise of the falling bombs and shells only aroused curiosity. Ferapóntov's wife, who till then had not ceased wailing under the shed, became quiet and with the baby in her arms went to the gate, listening to the sounds and looking in silence at the people.

The cook and a shop assistant came to the gate. With lively curiosity everyone tried to get a glimpse of the projectiles as they flew over their heads. Several people came round the corner talking eagerly.

"What force!" remarked one. "Knocked the roof and ceiling all to splinters!"

"Routed up the earth like a pig," said another.

"That's grand, it bucks one up!" laughed the first. "Lucky you jumped aside, or it would have wiped you out!"

Others joined those men and stopped and told how cannon balls had fallen on a house close to them. Meanwhile still more projectiles, now with the swift sinister whistle of a cannon ball, now with the agreeable intermittent whistle of a shell, flew over people's heads incessantly, but not one fell close by, they all flew over. Alpátych was getting into his trap. The innkeeper stood at the gate.

"What are you staring at?" he shouted to the cook, who in her red skirt, with sleeves rolled up, swinging her bare elbows, had stepped to the corner to listen to what was being said.

"What marvels!" she exclaimed, but hearing her master's voice she turned back, pulling down her tucked-up skirt.

Once more something whistled, but this time quite close, swooping downwards like a little bird; a flame flashed in the middle of the street, something exploded, and the street was shrouded in smoke.

"Scoundrel, what are you doing?" shouted the innkeeper, rushing to the cook.

At that moment the pitiful wailing of women was heard from different sides, the frightened baby began to cry, and people crowded silently with pale faces round the cook. The loudest sound in that crowd was her wailing.

"Oh-h-h! Dear souls, dear kind souls! Don't let me die! My good souls!..."

Five minutes later no one remained in the street. The cook, with her thigh broken by a shell splinter, had been carried into the kitchen. Alpátych, his coachman, Ferapóntov's wife and children and the house porter were all sitting in the cellar, listening. The roar of guns, the whistling of projectiles, and the piteous moaning of the cook, which rose above the other sounds, did not cease for a moment. The mistress rocked and hushed her baby and when anyone came into the cellar asked in a pathetic whisper what had become of her husband who had remained in the street. A shopman who entered told her that her husband had gone with others to the cathedral, whence they were fetching the wonder-working icon of Smolénsk.

Toward dusk the cannonade began to subside. Alpátych left the cellar and stopped in the doorway. The evening sky that had been so clear was clouded with smoke, through which, high up, the sickle of the new moon shone strangely. Now that the terrible din of the guns had ceased a hush seemed to reign over the town, broken only by the rustle of footsteps, the moaning, the distant cries, and the crackle of fires which seemed widespread everywhere. The cook's moans had now subsided. On two sides black curling clouds of smoke rose and spread from the fires. Through the streets soldiers in various uniforms walked or ran confusedly in different directions like ants from a ruined ant-hill. Several of them ran into Ferapóntov's yard before Alpátych's eyes. Alpátych went out to the gate. A retreating regiment, thronging and hurrying, blocked the street.

Noticing him, an officer said: "The town is being abandoned. Get away, get away!" and then, turning to the soldiers, shouted:

"I'll teach you to run into the yards!"

Alpátych went back to the house, called the coachman, and told him to set off. Ferapóntov's whole household came out too, following Alpátych and the coachman. The women, who had been silent till then, suddenly began to wail as they looked at the fires—the smoke and even the flames of which could be seen in the failing twilight—and as if in reply the same kind of lamentation was heard from other parts of the street. Inside the shed Alpátych and the coachman arranged the tangled reins and traces of their horses with trembling hands.

As Alpátych was driving out of the gate he saw some ten soldiers in Ferapóntov's open shop, talking loudly and filling their bags and knapsacks with flour and sunflower seeds. Just then Ferapóntov returned and entered his shop. On seeing the soldiers he was about to shout at them, but suddenly stopped and, clutching at his hair, burst into sobs and laughter:

"Loot everything, lads! Don't let those devils get it!" he cried, taking some bags of flour himself and throwing them into the street.

Some of the soldiers were frightened and ran away, others went on filling their bags. On seeing Alpátych, Ferapóntov turned to him:

"Russia is done for!" he cried. "Alpátych, I'll set the place on fire myself. We're done for!..." and Ferapóntov ran into the yard.

Soldiers were passing in a constant stream along the street blocking it completely, so that Alpátych could not pass out and had to wait. Ferapóntov's wife and children were also sitting in a cart waiting till it was possible to drive out.

Night had come. There were stars in the sky and the new moon shone out amid the smoke that screened it. On the sloping descent to the Dnieper Alpátych's cart and that of the innkeeper's wife, which were slowly moving amid the rows of soldiers and of other vehicles, had to stop. In a side street near the crossroads where the vehicles had stopped, a house and some shops were on fire. This fire was already burning itself out. The flames now died down and were lost in the black smoke, now suddenly flared up again brightly, lighting up with strange distinctness the faces of the people crowding at the crossroads. Black figures flitted about before the fire, and through the incessant crackling of the flames talking and shouting could be heard. Seeing that his trap would not be able to move on for some time, Alpátych got down and turned into the side street to look at the fire. Soldiers were continually rushing backwards and forwards near it, and he saw two of them and a man in a frieze coat dragging burning beams into another yard across the street, while others carried bundles of hay.

Alpátych went up to a large crowd standing before a high barn which was blazing briskly. The walls were all on fire and the back wall had fallen in, the wooden roof was collapsing, and the rafters were alight. The crowd was evidently watching for the roof to fall in, and Alpátych watched for it too.

"Alpátych!" a familiar voice suddenly hailed the old man.

"Mercy on us! Your excellency!" answered Alpátych, immediately recognizing the voice of his young prince.

Prince Andrew in his riding cloak, mounted on a black horse, was looking at Alpátych from the back of the crowd.

"Why are you here?" he asked.

"Your... your excellency," stammered Alpátych and broke into sobs. "Are we really lost? Master!..."

"Why are you here?" Prince Andrew repeated.

At that moment the flames flared up and showed his young master's pale worn face. Alpátych told how he had been sent there and how difficult it was to get away.

"Are we really quite lost, your excellency?" he asked again.

Prince Andrew without replying took out a notebook and raising his knee began writing in pencil on a page he tore out. He wrote to his sister:

"Smolénsk is being abandoned. Bald Hills will be occupied by the enemy within a week. Set off immediately for Moscow. Let me know at once when you will start. Send by special messenger to Usvyázh."

Having written this and given the paper to Alpátych, he told him how to arrange for departure of the prince, the princess, his son, and the boy's tutor, and how and where to let him know immediately. Before he had had time to finish giving these instructions, a chief of staff followed by a suite galloped up to him.

"You are a colonel?" shouted the chief of staff with a German accent, in a voice familiar to Prince Andrew. "Houses are set on fire in your presence and you stand by! What does this mean? You will answer for it!" shouted Berg, who was now assistant to the chief of staff of the commander of the left flank of the infantry of the first army, a place, as Berg said, "very agreeable and well *enévidence.*"

Prince Andrew looked at him and without replying went on speaking to Alpátych.

"So tell them that I shall await a reply till the tenth, and if by the tenth I don't receive news that they have all got away I shall have to throw up everything and come myself to Bald Hills."

"Prince," said Berg, recognizing Prince Andrew, "I only spoke because I have to obey orders, because I always do obey exactly.... You must please excuse me," he went on apologetically.

Something cracked in the flames. The fire died down for a moment and wreaths of black smoke rolled from under the roof. There was another terrible crash and something huge collapsed.

"Ou-rou-rou!" yelled the crowd, echoing the crash of the collapsing roof of the barn, the burning grain in which diffused a cakelike aroma all around. The flames flared up again, lighting the animated, delighted, exhausted faces of the spectators.

The man in the frieze coat raised his arms and shouted:

"It's fine, lads! Now it's raging... It's fine!"

"That's the owner himself," cried several voices.

"Well then," continued Prince Andrew to Alpátych, "report to them as I have told you"; and not replying a word to Berg who was now mute beside him, he touched his horse and rode down the side street.

CHAPTER V

From Smolénsk the troops continued to retreat, followed by the enemy. On the tenth of August the regiment Prince Andrew commanded was marching along the highroad past the avenue leading to Bald Hills. Heat and drought had continued for more than three weeks. Each day fleecy clouds floated across the sky and occasionally veiled the sun, but toward evening the sky cleared again and the sun set in reddish-brown mist. Heavy night dews alone refreshed the earth. The unreaped corn was scorched and shed its grain. The marshes dried up. The cattle lowed from hunger, finding no food on the sun-parched meadows. Only at night and in the forests while the dew lasted was there any freshness. But on the road, the highroad along which the troops marched, there was no such freshness even at night or when the road passed through the forest; the dew was imperceptible on the sandy dust churned up more than six inches deep. As soon as day dawned the march began. The artillery and baggage wagons moved noiselessly through the deep dust that rose to the very hubs of the wheels, and the infantry sank ankle-deep in that soft, choking, hot dust that never cooled even at night. Some of this dust was kneaded by the feet and wheels, while the rest rose and hung like a cloud over the troops, settling in eyes, ears, hair, and nostrils, and worst of all in the lungs of the men and beasts as they moved along that road. The higher the sun rose the higher rose that cloud of dust, and through the screen of its hot fine particles one could look with naked eye at the sun, which showed like a huge crimson ball in the unclouded sky. There was no wind, and the men choked in that motionless atmosphere. They marched with handkerchiefs tied over their noses and mouths. When they passed through a village they all rushed to the wells and fought for the water and drank it down to the mud.

Prince Andrew was in command of a regiment, and the management of that regiment, the welfare of the men and the necessity of receiving and giving orders, engrossed him. The burning of Smolénsk and its abandonment made an epoch in his life. A novel feeling of anger against the foe made him forget his own sorrow. He was entirely devoted to the affairs of his regiment and was considerate and kind to his men and officers. In the regiment they called him "our prince," were proud of him and loved him. But he was kind and gentle only to those of his regiment, to Timókhin and the like—people quite new to him, belonging to a different world and who could not know and understand his past. As soon as he came across a former acquaintance or anyone from the staff, he bristled up immediately and grew spiteful, ironical, and contemptuous. Everything that reminded him of his past was repugnant to him, and so in his relations with that former circle he confined himself to trying to do his duty and not to be unfair.

In truth everything presented itself in a dark and gloomy light to Prince Andrew, especially after the abandonment of Smolénsk on the sixth of August (he considered that it could and should have been defended) and after his sick father had had to flee to Moscow, abandoning to pillage his dearly beloved Bald Hills which he had built and peopled. But despite this, thanks to his regiment, Prince Andrew had something to think about entirely apart from general questions. Two days previously he had received news that his father, son, and sister had left for Moscow; and though there was nothing for him to do at Bald Hills, Prince Andrew with a characteristic desire to foment his own grief decided that he must ride there.

He ordered his horse to be saddled and, leaving his regiment on the march, rode to his father's estate where he had been born and spent his childhood. Riding past the pond where there used always to be dozens of women chattering as they rinsed their linen or beat it with wooden beetles, Prince Andrew noticed that there was not a soul about and that the little washing wharf, torn from its place and half submerged, was floating on its side in the middle of the pond. He rode to the keeper's lodge. No one was at the stone entrance gates of the drive and the door stood open. Grass had already begun to grow on the garden paths, and horses and calves were straying in the English park. Prince Andrew rode up to the hothouse; some of the glass panes were broken, and of the trees in tubs some were overturned and others dried up. He called for Tarás the gardener, but no one replied. Having gone round the corner of the hothouse to the ornamental garden, he saw that the carved garden fence was broken and branches of the plum trees had been torn off with the fruit. An old peasant whom Prince Andrew in his childhood had often seen at the gate was sitting on a green garden seat, plaiting a bast shoe.

He was deaf and did not hear Prince Andrew ride up. He was sitting on the seat the old prince used to like to sit on, and beside him strips of bast were hanging on the broken and withered branch of a magnolia.

Prince Andrew rode up to the house. Several limes in the old garden had been cut down and a piebald mare and her foal were wandering in front of the house among the rosebushes. The shutters were all closed, except at one window which was open. A little serf boy, seeing Prince Andrew, ran into the house. Alpátych, having sent his family away, was alone at Bald Hills and was sitting indoors reading the *Lives of the Saints*. On hearing that Prince Andrew had come, he went out with his spectacles on his nose, buttoning his coat, and, hastily stepping up, without a word began weeping and kissing Prince Andrew's knee.

Then, vexed at his own weakness, he turned away and began to report on the position of affairs. Everything precious and valuable had been removed to Boguchárovo. Seventy quarters of grain had also been carted away. The hay and the spring corn, of which Alpátych said there had been a remarkable crop that year, had been commandeered by the troops and mown down while still green. The peasants were ruined; some of them too had gone to Boguchárovo, only a few remained.

Without waiting to hear him out, Prince Andrew asked:

"When did my father and sister leave?" meaning when did they leave for Moscow.

Alpátych, understanding the question to refer to their departure for Boguchárovo, replied that they had left on the seventh and again went into details concerning the estate management, asking for instructions.

"Am I to let the troops have the oats, and to take a receipt for them? We have still six hundred quarters left," he inquired.

"What am I to say to him?" thought Prince Andrew, looking down on the old man's bald head shining in the sun and seeing by the expression on his face that the old man himself understood how untimely such questions were and only asked them to allay his grief.

"Yes, let them have it," replied Prince Andrew.

"If you noticed some disorder in the garden," said Alpátych, "it was impossible to prevent it. Three regiments have been here and spent the night, dragoons mostly. I took down the name and rank of their commanding officer, to hand in a complaint about it."

"Well, and what are you going to do? Will you stay here if the enemy occupies the place?" asked Prince Andrew.

Alpátych turned his face to Prince Andrew, looked at him, and suddenly with a solemn gesture raised his arm.

"He is my refuge! His will be done!" he exclaimed.

A group of bareheaded peasants was approaching across the meadow toward the prince.

"Well, good-by!" said Prince Andrew, bending over to Alpátych. "You must go away too, take away what you can and tell the serfs to go to the Ryazán estate or to the one near Moscow."

Alpátych clung to Prince Andrew's leg and burst into sobs. Gently disengaging himself, the prince spurred his horse and rode down the avenue at a gallop.

The old man was still sitting in the ornamental garden, like a fly impassive on the face of a loved one who is dead, tapping the last on which he was making the bast shoe, and two little girls, running out from the hot house carrying in their skirts plums they had plucked from the trees there, came upon Prince Andrew. On seeing the young master, the elder one with frightened look clutched her younger companion by the hand and hid with her behind a birch tree, not stopping to pick up some green plums they had dropped.

Prince Andrew turned away with startled haste, unwilling to let them see that they had been observed. He was sorry for the pretty frightened little girl, was afraid of looking at her, and yet felt an irresistible desire to do so. A new sensation of comfort and relief came over him when, seeing these girls, he realized the existence of other human interests entirely aloof from his own and just as legitimate as those that occupied him. Evidently these girls passionately desired one thing—to carry away and eat those green plums without being caught—and Prince Andrew shared their wish for the success of their enterprise. He could not resist looking at them once more. Believing their danger past, they sprang from their ambush and, chirruping something in their shrill little voices and holding up their skirts, their bare little sunburned feet scampered merrily and quickly across the meadow grass.

Prince Andrew was somewhat refreshed by having ridden off the dusty highroad along which the troops were moving. But not far from Bald Hills he again came out on the road and overtook his regiment at its halting place by the dam of a small pond. It was past one o'clock. The sun, a red ball through the dust, burned and scorched his back intolerably through his black coat. The dust always hung motionless above the buzz of talk that came from the resting troops. There was no wind. As he crossed the dam Prince Andrew smelled the ooze and freshness of the pond. He longed to get into that water, however dirty it might be, and he glanced round at the pool from whence came sounds of shrieks and laughter. The small, muddy, green pond had risen visibly more than a foot, flooding the dam, because it was full of the naked white bodies of soldiers with brick-red hands, necks, and faces, who were splashing about in it. All this naked white human flesh, laughing and shrieking, floundered about in that dirty pool like carp stuffed into a watering can, and the suggestion of merriment in that floundering mass rendered it specially pathetic.

One fair-haired young soldier of the third company, whom Prince Andrew knew and who had a strap round the calf of one leg, crossed himself, stepped back to get a good run, and plunged into the water; another, a dark noncommissioned officer who was always shaggy, stood up to his waist in the water joyfully wriggling his muscular figure and snorted with satisfaction as he poured the water over his head with hands blackened to the wrists. There were sounds of men slapping one another, yelling, and puffing.

Everywhere on the bank, on the dam, and in the pond, there was healthy, white, muscular flesh. The officer, Timókhin, with his red little nose, standing on the dam wiping himself with a towel, felt confused at seeing the prince, but made up his mind to address him nevertheless.

"It's very nice, your excellency! Wouldn't you like to?" said he.

"It's dirty," replied Prince Andrew, making a grimace.

"We'll clear it out for you in a minute," said Timókhin, and, still undressed, ran off to clear the men out of the pond.

"The prince wants to bathe."

"What prince? Ours?" said many voices, and the men were in such haste to clear out that the prince could hardly stop them. He decided that he would rather wash himself with water in the barn.

"Flesh, bodies, cannon fodder!" he thought, and he looked at his own naked body and shuddered, not from cold but from a sense of disgust and horror he did not himself understand, aroused by the sight of that immense number of bodies splashing about in the dirty pond.

On the seventh of August Prince Bagratión wrote as follows from his quarters at Mikháylovna on the Smolénsk road:

Dear Count AléxisAndréevich—(He was writing to Arakchéev but knew that his letter would be read by the Emperor, and therefore weighed every word in it to the best of his ability.)

I expect the Minister (Barclay de Tolly) has already reported the abandonment of Smolénsk to the enemy. It is pitiable and sad, and the whole army is in despair that this most important place has been wantonly abandoned. I, for my part, begged him personally most urgently and finally wrote him, but nothing would induce him to consent. I swear to you on my honor that Napoleon was in such a fix as never before and might have lost half his army but could not have taken Smolénsk. Our troops fought, and are fighting, as never before. With fifteen thousand men I held the enemy at bay for thirty-five hours and beat him; but *he* would not hold out even for fourteen hours. It is disgraceful, a stain on our army, and as for him, he ought, it seems to me, not to live. If he reports that our losses were great, it is not true; perhaps about four thousand, not more, and not even that; but even were they ten thousand, that's war! But the enemy has lost masses....

What would it have cost him to hold out for another two days? They would have had to retire of their own accord, for they had no water for men or horses. He gave me his word he would not retreat, but suddenly sent instructions that he was retiring that night. We cannot fight in this way, or we may soon bring the enemy to Moscow....

There is a rumor that you are thinking of peace. God forbid that you should make peace after all our sacrifices and such insane retreats! You would set all Russia against you and everyone of us would feel ashamed to wear the uniform. If it has come to this—we must fight as long as Russia can and as long as there are men able to stand....

One man ought to be in command, and not two. Your Minister may perhaps be good as a Minister, but as a general he is not merely bad but execrable, yet to him is entrusted the fate of our whole country.... I am really frantic with vexation; forgive my writing boldly. It is clear that the man who advocates the conclusion of a peace, and that the Minister should command the army, does not love our sovereign and desires the ruin of us all. So I write you frankly: call out the militia. For the Minister is leading these visitors after him to Moscow in a most masterly way. The whole army feels great suspicion of the Imperial aide-de-camp Wolzogen. He is said to be more Napoleon's man than ours, and he is always advising the Minister. I am not merely civil to him but obey him like a corporal, though I am his senior. This is painful, but, loving my benefactor and sovereign, I submit. Only I am sorry for the Emperor that he entrusts our fine army to such as he. Consider that on our retreat we have lost by fatigue and left in the hospital more than fifteen thousand men, and had we attacked this would not have happened. Tell me, for God's sake, what will Russia, our mother Russia, say to our being so frightened, and why are we abandoning our good and gallant Fatherland to such rabble and implanting feelings of hatred and shame in all our subjects? What are we scared at and of whom are we afraid? I am not to blame that the Minister is vacillating, a coward, dense, dilatory, and has all bad qualities. The whole army bewails it and calls down curses upon him....

CHAPTER VI

Among the innumerable categories applicable to the phenomena of human life one may discriminate between those in which substance prevails and those in which form prevails. To the latter—as distinguished from village, country, provincial, or even Moscow life—we may allot Petersburg life, and especially the life of its salons. That life of the salons is unchanging. Since the year 1805 we had made peace and had again quarreled with Bonaparte and had made constitutions and unmade them again, but the salons of Anna Pávlovna and Hélène remained just as they had been—the one seven and the other five years before. At Anna Pávlovna's they talked with perplexity of Bonaparte's successes just as before and saw in them and in the subservience shown to him by the European sovereigns a malicious conspiracy, the sole object of which was to cause unpleasantness and anxiety to the court circle of which Anna Pávlovna was the representative. And in Hélène's salon, which Rumyántsev himself honored with his visits, regarding Hélène as a remarkably intelligent woman, they talked with the same ecstasy in 1812 as in 1808 of the "great nation" and the "great man," and regretted our rupture with France, a rupture which, according to them, ought to be promptly terminated by peace.

Of late, since the Emperor's return from the army, there had been some excitement in these conflicting salon circles and some demonstrations of hostility to one another, but each camp retained its own tendency. In Anna Pávlovna's circle only those Frenchmen were admitted who were deep-rooted legitimists, and patriotic views were expressed to the effect that one ought not to go to the French theater and that to maintain the French troupe was costing the government as much as a whole army corps. The progress of the war was eagerly followed, and only the reports most flattering to our army were circulated. In the French circle of Hélène and Rumyántsev the reports of the cruelty of the enemy and of the war were contradicted and all Napoleon's attempts at conciliation were discussed. In that circle they discountenanced those who advised hurried preparations for a removal to Kazán of the court and the girls' educational establishments under the patronage of the Dowager Empress. In Hélène's circle the war in general was regarded as a series of formal demonstrations which would very soon end in peace, and the view prevailed expressed by Bilíbin—who now in Petersburg was quite at home in Hélène's house, which every clever man was obliged to visit—that not by gunpowder but by those who invented it would matters be settled. In that circle the Moscow enthusiasm—news of which had reached Petersburg simultaneously with the Emperor's return—was ridiculed sarcastically and very cleverly, though with much caution.

Anna Pávlovna's circle on the contrary was enraptured by this enthusiasm and spoke of it as Plutarch speaks of the deeds of the ancients. Prince Vasíli, who still occupied his former important posts, formed a connecting link between these two circles. He visited his "good friend Anna Pávlovna" as well as his daughter's "diplomatic salon," and often in his constant comings and goings between the two camps became confused and said at Hélène's what he should have said at Anna Pávlovna's and vice versa.

Soon after the Emperor's return Prince Vasíli in a conversation about the war at Anna Pávlovna's severely condemned Barclay de Tolly, but was undecided as to who ought to be appointed commander in chief. One of the visitors, usually spoken of as "a man of great merit," having described how he had that day seen Kutúzov, the newly chosen chief of the Petersburg militia, presiding over the enrollment of recruits at the Treasury, cautiously ventured to suggest that Kutúzov would be the man to satisfy all requirements.

Anna Pávlovna remarked with a melancholy smile that Kutúzov had done nothing but cause the Emperor annoyance.

"I have talked and talked at the Assembly of the Nobility," Prince Vasíli interrupted, "but they did not listen to me. I told them his election as chief of the militia would not please the Emperor. They did not listen to me.

"It's all this mania for opposition," he went on. "And who for? It is all because we want to ape the foolish enthusiasm of those Muscovites," Prince Vasíli continued, forgetting for a moment that though at Hélène's one had to ridicule the Moscow enthusiasm, at Anna Pávlovna's one had to be ecstatic about it. But he retrieved his mistake at once. "Now, is it suitable that Count Kutúzov, the oldest general in Russia, should preside at that tribunal? He will get nothing for his pains! How could they make a man commander in chief who cannot mount a horse, who drops asleep at a council, and has the very worst morals! A good reputation he made for himself at Bucharest! I don't speak of his capacity as a general, but at a time like this how they appoint a decrepit, blind old man, positively blind? A fine idea to have a blind general! He can't see anything. To play blindman's buff? He can't see at all!"

No one replied to his remarks.

This was quite correct on the twenty-fourth of July. But on the twenty-ninth of July Kutúzov received the title of Prince. This might indicate a wish to get rid of him, and therefore Prince Vasíli's opinion continued to be correct though he was not now in any hurry to express it. But on the eighth of August a committee, consisting of Field Marshal Saltykóv, Arakchéev, Vyazmítinov, Lopukhín, and Kochubéy met to consider the progress of the war. This committee came to the conclusion that our failures were due to a want of unity in the command and though the members of the committee were aware of the Emperor's dislike of Kutúzov, after a short deliberation they agreed to advise his appointment as commander in chief. That same day Kutúzov was appointed commander in chief with full powers over the armies and over the whole region occupied by them.

On the ninth of August Prince Vasíli at Anna Pávlovna's again met the "man of great merit." The latter was very attentive to Anna Pávlovna because he wanted to be appointed director of one of the educational establishments for young ladies. Prince Vasíli entered the room with the air of a happy conqueror who has attained the object of his desires.

"Well, have you heard the great news? Prince Kutúzov is field marshal! All dissensions are at an end! I am so glad, so delighted! At last we have a man!" said he, glancing sternly and significantly round at everyone in the drawing room.

The "man of great merit," despite his desire to obtain the post of director, could not refrain from reminding Prince Vasíli of his former opinion. Though this was impolite to Prince Vasíli in Anna Pávlovna's drawing room, and also to Anna Pávlovna herself who had received the news with delight, he could not resist the temptation.

"But, Prince, they say he is blind!" said he, reminding Prince Vasíli of his own words.

"Eh? Nonsense! He sees well enough," said Prince Vasíli rapidly, in a deep voice and with a slight cough—the voice and cough with which he was wont to dispose of all difficulties.

"He sees well enough," he added. "And what I am so pleased about," he went on, "is that our sovereign has given him full powers over all the armies and the whole region—powers no commander in chief ever had before. He is a second autocrat," he concluded with a victorious smile.

"God grant it! God grant it!" said Anna Pávlovna.

The "man of great merit," who was still a novice in court circles, wishing to flatter Anna Pávlovna by defending her former position on this question, observed:

"It is said that the Emperor was reluctant to give Kutúzov those powers. They say he blushed like a girl to whom *Joconde* is read, when he said to Kutúzov: 'Your Emperor and the Fatherland award you this honor.'"

"Perhaps the heart took no part in that speech," said Anna Pávlovna.

"Oh, no, no!" warmly rejoined Prince Vasíli, who would not now yield Kutúzov to anyone; in his opinion Kutúzov was not only admirable himself, but was adored by everybody. "No, that's impossible," said he, "for our sovereign appreciated him so highly before."

"God grant only that Prince Kutúzov assumes real power and does not allow *anyone* to put a spoke in his wheel," observed Anna Pávlovna.

Understanding at once to whom she alluded, Prince Vasíli said in a whisper:

"I know for a fact that Kutúzov made it an absolute condition that the Tsarévich should not be with the army. Do you know what he said to the Emperor?"

And Prince Vasíli repeated the words supposed to have been spoken by Kutúzov to the Emperor. "I can neither punish him if he does wrong nor reward him if he does right."

"Oh, a very wise man is Prince Kutúzov! I have known him a long time!"

"They even say," remarked the "man of great merit" who did not yet possess courtly tact, "that his excellency made it an express condition that the sovereign himself should not be with the army."

As soon as he said this both Prince Vasíli and Anna Pávlovna turned away from him and glanced sadly at one another with a sigh at his naïveté.

CHAPTER VII

While this was taking place in Petersburg the French had already passed Smolénsk and were drawing nearer and nearer to Moscow. Napoleon's historian Thiers, like other of his historians, trying to justify his hero says that he was drawn to the walls of Moscow against his will. He is as right as other historians who look for the explanation of historic events in the will of one man; he is as right as the Russian historians who maintain that Napoleon was drawn to Moscow by the skill of the Russian commanders. Here besides the law of retrospection, which regards all the past as a preparation for events that subsequently occur, the law of reciprocity comes in, confusing the whole matter. A good chessplayer having lost a game is sincerely convinced that his loss resulted from a mistake he made and looks for that mistake in the opening, but forgets that at each stage of the game there were similar mistakes and that none of his moves were perfect. He only notices the mistake to which he pays attention, because his opponent took advantage of it. How much more complex than this is the game of war, which occurs under certain limits of time, and where it is not one will that manipulates lifeless objects, but everything results from innumerable conflicts of various wills!

After Smolénsk Napoleon sought a battle beyond Dorogobúzh at Vyázma, and then at Tsárevo-Zaymíshche, but it happened that owing to a conjunction of innumerable circumstances the Russians could not give battle till they reached Borodinó, seventy miles from Moscow. From Vyázma Napoleon ordered a direct advance on Moscow.

Moscou, la capitaleasiatique de ce grand empire, la villesacrée des peuplesd'Alexandre, Moscou avec sesinnombrableséglisesenforme de pagodes chinoises, * this Moscow gave Napoleon's imagination no rest. On the march from Vyázma to Tsárevo-Zaymíshche he rode his light bay bobtailed ambler accompanied by his Guards, his bodyguard, his pages, and aides-de-camp. Berthier, his chief of staff, dropped behind to question a Russian prisoner captured by the cavalry. Followed by Lelorgned'Ideville, an interpreter, he overtook Napoleon at a gallop and reined in his horse with an amused expression.

* "Moscow, the Asiatic capital of this great empire, the sacred city of Alexander's people, Moscow with its innumerable churches shaped like Chinese pagodas."

"Well?" asked Napoleon.

"One of Plátov's Cossacks says that Plátov's corps is joining up with the main army and that Kutúzov has been appointed commander in chief. He is a very shrewd and garrulous fellow."

Napoleon smiled and told them to give the Cossack a horse and bring the man to him. He wished to talk to him himself. Several adjutants galloped off, and an hour later, Lavrúshka, the serf Denísov had handed over to Rostóv, rode up to Napoleon in an orderly's jacket and on a French cavalry saddle, with a merry, and tipsy face. Napoleon told him to ride by his side and began questioning him.

"You are a Cossack?"

"Yes, a Cossack, your Honor."

"The Cossack, not knowing in what company he was, for Napoleon's plain appearance had nothing about it that would reveal to an Oriental mind the presence of a monarch, talked with extreme familiarity of the incidents of the war," says Thiers, narrating this episode. In reality Lavrúshka, having got drunk the day before and left his master dinnerless, had been whipped and sent to the village in quest of chickens, where he engaged in looting till the French took him prisoner. Lavrúshka was one of those coarse, bare-faced lackeys who have seen all sorts of things, consider it necessary to do everything in a mean and cunning way, are ready to render any sort of service to their master, and are keen at guessing their master's baser impulses, especially those prompted by vanity and pettiness.

Finding himself in the company of Napoleon, whose identity he had easily and surely recognized, Lavrúshka was not in the least abashed but merely did his utmost to gain his new master's favor.

He knew very well that this was Napoleon, but Napoleon's presence could no more intimidate him than Rostóv's, or a sergeant major's with the rods, would have done, for he had nothing that either the sergeant major or Napoleon could deprive him of.

So he rattled on, telling all the gossip he had heard among the orderlies. Much of it true. But when Napoleon asked him whether the Russians thought they would beat Bonaparte or not, Lavrúshka screwed up his eyes and considered.

In this question he saw subtle cunning, as men of his type see cunning in everything, so he frowned and did not answer immediately.

"It's like this," he said thoughtfully, "if there's a battle soon, yours will win. That's right. But if three days pass, then after that, well, then that same battle will not soon be over."

Lelorgned'Ideville smilingly interpreted this speech to Napoleon thus: "If a battle takes place within the next three days the French will win, but if later, God knows what will happen." Napoleon did not smile, though he was evidently in high good humor, and he ordered these words to be repeated.

Lavrúshka noticed this and to entertain him further, pretending not to know who Napoleon was, added:

"We know that you have Bonaparte and that he has beaten everybody in the world, but we are a different matter..."—without knowing why or how this bit of boastful patriotism slipped out at the end.

The interpreter translated these words without the last phrase, and Bonaparte smiled. "The young Cossack made his mighty interlocutor smile," says Thiers. After riding a few paces in silence, Napoleon turned to Berthier and said he wished to see how the news that he was talking to the Emperor himself, to that very Emperor who had written his immortally victorious name on the Pyramids, would affect this *enfant du Don.* *

* "Child of the Don."

The fact was accordingly conveyed to Lavrúshka.

War and Peace

Lavrúshka, understanding that this was done to perplex him and that Napoleon expected him to be frightened, to gratify his new masters promptly pretended to be astonished and awe-struck, opened his eyes wide, and assumed the expression he usually put on when taken to be whipped. "As soon as Napoleon's interpreter had spoken," says Thiers, "the Cossack, seized by amazement, did not utter another word, but rode on, his eyes fixed on the conqueror whose fame had reached him across the steppes of the East. All his loquacity was suddenly arrested and replaced by a naïve and silent feeling of admiration. Napoleon, after making the Cossack a present, had him set free like a bird restored to its native fields."

Napoleon rode on, dreaming of the Moscow that so appealed to his imagination, and "the bird restored to its native fields" galloped to our outposts, inventing on the way all that had not taken place but that he meant to relate to his comrades. What had really taken place he did not wish to relate because it seemed to him not worth telling. He found the Cossacks, inquired for the regiment operating with Plátov's detachment and by evening found his master, Nicholas Rostóv, quartered at Yankóvo. Rostóv was just mounting to go for a ride round the neighboring villages with Ilyín; he let Lavrúshka have another horse and took him along with him.

CHAPTER VIII

Princess Mary was not in Moscow and out of danger as Prince Andrew supposed.

After the return of Alpátych from Smolénsk the old prince suddenly seemed to awake as from a dream. He ordered the militiamen to be called up from the villages and armed, and wrote a letter to the commander in chief informing him that he had resolved to remain at Bald Hills to the last extremity and to defend it, leaving to the commander in chief's discretion to take measures or not for the defense of Bald Hills, where one of Russia's oldest generals would be captured or killed, and he announced to his household that he would remain at Bald Hills.

But while himself remaining, he gave instructions for the departure of the princess and Dessalles with the little prince to Boguchárovo and thence to Moscow. Princess Mary, alarmed by her father's feverish and sleepless activity after his previous apathy, could not bring herself to leave him alone and for the first time in her life ventured to disobey him. She refused to go away and her father's fury broke over her in a terrible storm. He repeated every injustice he had ever inflicted on her. Trying to convict her, he told her she had worn him out, had caused his quarrel with his son, had harbored nasty suspicions of him, making it the object of her life to poison his existence, and he drove her from his study telling her that if she did not go away it was all the same to him. He declared that he did not wish to remember her existence and warned her not to dare to let him see her. The fact that he did not, as she had feared, order her to be carried away by force but only told her not to let him see her cheered Princess Mary. She knew it was a proof that in the depth of his soul he was glad she was remaining at home and had not gone away.

The morning after little Nicholas had left, the old prince donned his full uniform and prepared to visit the commander in chief. His *calèche* was already at the door. Princess Mary saw him walk out of the house in his uniform wearing all his orders and go down the garden to review his armed peasants and domestic serfs. She sat by the window listening to his voice which reached her from the garden. Suddenly several men came running up the avenue with frightened faces.

Princess Mary ran out to the porch, down the flower-bordered path, and into the avenue. A large crowd of militiamen and domestics were moving toward her, and in their midst several men were supporting by the armpits and dragging along a little old man in a uniform and decorations. She ran up to him and, in the play of the sunlight that fell in small round spots through the shade of the lime-tree avenue, could not be sure what change there was in his face. All she could see was that his former stern and determined expression had altered to one of timidity and submission. On seeing his daughter he moved his helpless lips and made a hoarse sound. It was impossible to make out what he wanted. He was lifted up, carried to his study, and laid on the very couch he had so feared of late.

The doctor, who was fetched that same night, bled him and said that the prince had had a seizure paralyzing his right side.

It was becoming more and more dangerous to remain at Bald Hills, and next day they moved the prince to Boguchárovo, the doctor accompanying him.

By the time they reached Boguchárovo, Dessalles and the little prince had already left for Moscow.

For three weeks the old prince lay stricken by paralysis in the new house Prince Andrew had built at Boguchárovo, ever in the same state, getting neither better nor worse. He was unconscious and lay like a distorted corpse. He muttered unceasingly, his eyebrows and lips twitching, and it was impossible to tell whether he understood what was going on around him or not. One thing was certain—that he was suffering and wished to say something. But what it was, no one could tell: it might be some caprice of a sick and half-crazy man, or it might relate to public affairs, or possibly to family concerns.

The doctor said this restlessness did not mean anything and was due to physical causes; but Princess Mary thought he wished to tell her something, and the fact that her presence always increased his restlessness confirmed her opinion.

He was evidently suffering both physically and mentally. There was no hope of recovery. It was impossible for him to travel, it would not do to let him die on the road. "Would it not be better if the end did come, the very end?" Princess Mary sometimes thought. Night and day, hardly sleeping at all, she watched him and, terrible to say, often watched him not with hope of finding signs of improvement but wishing to find symptoms of the approach of the end.

Strange as it was to her to acknowledge this feeling in herself, yet there it was. And what seemed still more terrible to her was that since her father's illness began (perhaps even sooner, when she stayed with him expecting something to happen), all the personal desires and hopes that had been forgotten or sleeping within her had awakened. Thoughts that had not entered her mind for years—thoughts of a life free from the fear of her father, and even the possibility of love and of family happiness—floated continually in her imagination like temptations of the devil. Thrust them aside as she would, questions continually recurred to her as to how she would order her life now, after *that*. These were temptations of the devil and Princess Mary knew it. She knew that the sole weapon against *him* was prayer, and she tried to pray. She assumed an attitude of prayer, looked at the icons, repeated the words of a prayer, but she could not pray. She felt that a different world had now taken possession of her—the life of a world of strenuous and free activity, quite opposed to the spiritual world in which till now she had been confined and in which her greatest comfort had been prayer. She could not pray, could not weep, and worldly cares took possession of her.

It was becoming dangerous to remain in Boguchárovo. News of the approach of the French came from all sides, and in one village, ten miles from Boguchárovo, a homestead had been looted by French marauders.

The doctor insisted on the necessity of moving the prince; the provincial Marshal of the Nobility sent an official to Princess Mary to persuade her to get away as quickly as possible, and the head of the rural police having come to Boguchárovo urged the same thing, saying that the French were only some twenty-five miles away, that

French proclamations were circulating in the villages, and that if the princess did not take her father away before the fifteenth, he could not answer for the consequences.

The princess decided to leave on the fifteenth. The cares of preparation and giving orders, for which everyone came to her, occupied her all day. She spent the night of the fourteenth as usual, without undressing, in the room next to the one where the prince lay. Several times, waking up, she heard his groans and muttering, the creak of his bed, and the steps of Tíkhon and the doctor when they turned him over. Several times she listened at the door, and it seemed to her that his mutterings were louder than usual and that they turned him over oftener. She could not sleep and several times went to the door and listened, wishing to enter but not deciding to do so. Though he did not speak, Princess Mary saw and knew how unpleasant every sign of anxiety on his account was to him. She had noticed with what dissatisfaction he turned from the look she sometimes involuntarily fixed on him. She knew that her going in during the night at an unusual hour would irritate him.

But never had she felt so grieved for him or so much afraid of losing him. She recalled all her life with him and in every word and act of his found an expression of his love of her. Occasionally amid these memories temptations of the devil would surge into her imagination: thoughts of how things would be after his death, and how her new, liberated life would be ordered. But she drove these thoughts away with disgust. Toward morning he became quiet and she fell asleep.

She woke late. That sincerity which often comes with waking showed her clearly what chiefly concerned her about her father's illness. On waking she listened to what was going on behind the door and, hearing him groan, said to herself with a sigh that things were still the same.

"But what could have happened? What did I want? I want his death!" she cried with a feeling of loathing for herself.

She washed, dressed, said her prayers, and went out to the porch. In front of it stood carriages without horses and things were being packed into the vehicles.

It was a warm, gray morning. Princess Mary stopped at the porch, still horrified by her spiritual baseness and trying to arrange her thoughts before going to her father. The doctor came downstairs and went out to her.

"He is a little better today," said he. "I was looking for you. One can make out something of what he is saying. His head is clearer. Come in, he is asking for you...."

Princess Mary's heart beat so violently at this news that she grew pale and leaned against the wall to keep from falling. To see him, talk to him, feel his eyes on her now that her whole soul was overflowing with those dreadful, wicked temptations, was a torment of joy and terror.

"Come," said the doctor.

Princess Mary entered her father's room and went up to his bed. He was lying on his back propped up high, and his small bony hands with their knotted purple veins were lying on the quilt; his left eye gazed straight before him, his right eye was awry, and his brows and lips motionless. He seemed altogether so thin, small, and pathetic. His face seemed to have shriveled or melted; his features had grown smaller. Princess Mary went up and kissed his hand. His left hand pressed hers so that she understood that he had long been waiting for her to come. He twitched her hand, and his brows and lips quivered angrily.

She looked at him in dismay trying to guess what he wanted of her. When she changed her position so that his left eye could see her face he calmed down, not taking his eyes off her for some seconds. Then his lips and tongue moved, sounds came, and he began to speak, gazing timidly and imploringly at her, evidently afraid that she might not understand.

Straining all her faculties Princess Mary looked at him. The comic efforts with which he moved his tongue made her drop her eyes and with difficulty repress the sobs that rose to her throat. He said something, repeating the same words several times. She could not understand them, but tried to guess what he was saying and inquiringly repeated the words he uttered.

"Mmm...ar...ate...ate..." he repeated several times.

It was quite impossible to understand these sounds. The doctor thought he had guessed them, and inquiringly repeated: *"Mary, are you afraid?"* The prince shook his head, again repeated the same sounds.

"My mind, my mind aches?" questioned Princess Mary.

He made a mumbling sound in confirmation of this, took her hand, and began pressing it to different parts of his breast as if trying to find the right place for it.

"Always thoughts... about you... thoughts..." he then uttered much more clearly than he had done before, now that he was sure of being understood.

Princess Mary pressed her head against his hand, trying to hide her sobs and tears.

He moved his hand over her hair.

"I have been calling you all night..." he brought out.

"If only I had known..." she said through her tears. "I was afraid to come in."

He pressed her hand.

"Weren't you asleep?"

"No, I did not sleep," said Princess Mary, shaking her head.

Unconsciously imitating her father, she now tried to express herself as he did, as much as possible by signs, and her tongue too seemed to move with difficulty.

"Dear one... Dearest..." Princess Mary could not quite make out what he had said, but from his look it was clear that he had uttered a tender caressing word such as he had never used to her before. "Why didn't you come in?"

"And I was wishing for his death!" thought Princess Mary.

He was silent awhile.

"Thank you... daughter dear!... for all, for all... forgive!... thank you!... forgive!... thank you!..." and tears began to flow from his eyes. "Call Andrew!" he said suddenly, and a childish, timid expression of doubt showed itself on his face as he spoke.

He himself seemed aware that his demand was meaningless. So at least it seemed to Princess Mary.

"I have a letter from him," she replied.

He glanced at her with timid surprise.

"Where is he?"

"He's with the army, Father, at Smolénsk."

He closed his eyes and remained silent a long time. Then as if in answer to his doubts and to confirm the fact that now he understood and remembered everything, he nodded his head and reopened his eyes.

"Yes," he said, softly and distinctly. "Russia has perished. They've destroyed her."

And he began to sob, and again tears flowed from his eyes. Princess Mary could no longer restrain herself and wept while she gazed at his face.

Again he closed his eyes. His sobs ceased, he pointed to his eyes, and Tíkhon, understanding him, wiped away the tears.

Then he again opened his eyes and said something none of them could understand for a long time, till at last Tíkhon understood and repeated it. Princess Mary had sought the meaning of his words in the mood in which he had just been speaking. She thought he was speaking of Russia, or Prince Andrew, of herself, of his grandson, or of his own death, and so she could not guess his words.

"Put on your white dress. I like it," was what he said.

Having understood this Princess Mary sobbed still louder, and the doctor taking her arm led her out to the veranda, soothing her and trying to persuade her to prepare for her journey. When she had left the room the prince again began speaking about his son, about the war, and about the Emperor, angrily twitching his brows and raising his hoarse voice, and then he had a second and final stroke.

Princess Mary stayed on the veranda. The day had cleared, it was hot and sunny. She could understand nothing, think of nothing and feel nothing, except passionate love for her father, love such as she thought she had never felt till that moment. She ran out sobbing into the garden and as far as the pond, along the avenues of young lime trees Prince Andrew had planted.

"Yes... I... I... I wished for his death! Yes, I wanted it to end quicker.... I wished to be at peace.... And what will become of me? What use will peace be when he is no longer here?" Princess Mary murmured, pacing the garden with hurried steps and pressing her hands to her bosom which heaved with convulsive sobs.

When she had completed the tour of the garden, which brought her again to the house, she saw Mademoiselle Bourienne—who had remained at Boguchárovo and did not wish to leave it—coming toward her with a stranger. This was the Marshal of the Nobility of the district, who had come personally to point out to the princess the necessity for her prompt departure. Princess Mary listened without understanding him; she led him to the house, offered him lunch, and sat down with him. Then, excusing herself, she went to the door of the old prince's room. The doctor came out with an agitated face and said she could not enter.

"Go away, Princess! Go away... go away!"

She returned to the garden and sat down on the grass at the foot of the slope by the pond, where no one could see her. She did not know how long she had been there when she was aroused by the sound of a woman's footsteps running along the path. She rose and saw Dunyásha her maid, who was evidently looking for her, and who stopped suddenly as if in alarm on seeing her mistress.

"Please come, Princess... The Prince," said Dunyásha in a breaking voice.

"Immediately, I'm coming, I'm coming!" replied the princess hurriedly, not giving Dunyásha time to finish what she was saying, and trying to avoid seeing the girl she ran toward the house.

"Princess, it's God's will! You must be prepared for everything," said the Marshal, meeting her at the house door.

"Let me alone; it's not true!" she cried angrily to him.

The doctor tried to stop her. She pushed him aside and ran to her father's door. "Why are these people with frightened faces stopping me? I don't want any of them! And what are they doing here?" she thought. She opened the door and the bright daylight in that previously darkened room startled her. In the room were her nurse and other women. They all drew back from the bed, making way for her. He was still lying on the bed as before, but the stern expression of his quiet face made Princess Mary stop short on the threshold.

"No, he's not dead—it's impossible!" she told herself and approached him, and repressing the terror that seized her, she pressed her lips to his cheek. But she stepped back immediately. All the force of the tenderness she had been feeling for him vanished instantly and was replaced by a feeling of horror at what lay there before her. "No, he is no more! He is not, but here where he was is something unfamiliar and hostile, some dreadful, terrifying, and repellent mystery!" And hiding her face in her hands, Princess Mary sank into the arms of the doctor, who held her up.

In the presence of Tíkhon and the doctor the women washed what had been the prince, tied his head up with a handkerchief that the mouth should not stiffen while open, and with another handkerchief tied together the legs that were already spreading apart. Then they dressed him in uniform with his decorations and placed his shriveled little body on a table. Heaven only knows who arranged all this and when, but it all got done as if of its own accord. Toward night candles were burning round his coffin, a pall was spread over it, the floor was strewn with sprays of juniper, a printed band was tucked in under his shriveled head, and in a corner of the room sat a chanter reading the psalms.

Just as horses shy and snort and gather about a dead horse, so the inmates of the house and strangers crowded into the drawing room round the coffin—the Marshal, the village Elder, peasant women—and all with fixed and frightened eyes, crossing themselves, bowed and kissed the old prince's cold and stiffened hand.

CHAPTER IX

Until Prince Andrew settled in Boguchárovo its owners had always been absentees, and its peasants were of quite a different character from those of Bald Hills. They differed from them in speech, dress, and disposition. They were called steppe peasants. The old prince used to approve of them for their endurance at work when they came to Bald Hills to help with the harvest. or to dig ponds and ditches, but he disliked them for their boorishness.

Prince Andrew's last stay at Boguchárovo, when he introduced hospitals and schools and reduced the quitrent the peasants had to pay, had not softened their disposition but had on the contrary strengthened in them the traits of character the old prince called boorishness. Various obscure rumors were always current among them: at one time a rumor that they would all be enrolled as Cossacks; at another of a new religion to which they were all to be converted; then of some proclamation of the Tsar's and of an oath to the Tsar Paul in 1797 (in connection with which it was rumored that freedom had been granted them but the landowners had stopped it), then of Peter Fëdorovich's return to the throne in seven years' time, when everything would be made free and so "simple" that there would be no restrictions. Rumors of the war with Bonaparte and his invasion were connected in their minds with the same sort of vague notions of Antichrist, the end of the world, and "pure freedom."

In the vicinity of Boguchárovo were large villages belonging to the crown or to owners whose serfs paid quitrent and could work where they pleased. There were very few resident landlords in the neighborhood and also very few domestic or literate serfs, and in the lives of the peasantry of those parts the mysterious undercurrents in the life of the Russian people, the causes and meaning of which are so baffling to contemporaries, were more clearly and strongly noticeable than among others. One instance, which had occurred some twenty years before, was a movement among the peasants to emigrate to some unknown "warm rivers." Hundreds of peasants, among them the Boguchárovo folk, suddenly began selling their cattle and moving in whole families toward the southeast. As birds migrate to somewhere beyond the sea, so these men with their wives and children streamed to the southeast, to parts where none of them had ever been. They set off in caravans, bought their freedom one by one or ran away, and drove or walked toward the "warm rivers." Many of them were punished, some sent to Siberia, many died of cold and hunger on the road, many returned of their own accord, and the movement died down of itself just as it had sprung up, without apparent reason. But such undercurrents still existed among the people and gathered new forces ready to manifest themselves just as strangely, unexpectedly, and at the same time simply, naturally, and forcibly. Now in 1812, to anyone living in close touch with these people it was apparent that these undercurrents were acting strongly and nearing an eruption.

Alpátych, who had reached Boguchárovo shortly before the old prince's death, noticed an agitation among the peasants, and that contrary to what was happening in the Bald Hills district, where over a radius of forty miles all the peasants were moving away and leaving their villages to be devastated by the Cossacks, the peasants in the steppe region round Boguchárovo were, it was rumored, in touch with the French, received leaflets from them that passed from hand to hand, and did not migrate. He learned from domestic serfs loyal to him that the peasant Karp, who possessed great influence in the village commune and had recently been away driving a government transport, had returned with news that the Cossacks were destroying deserted villages, but that the French did not harm them. Alpátych also knew that on the previous day another peasant had even brought from the village of Visloúkhovo, which was occupied by the French, a proclamation by a French general that no harm would be done to the inhabitants, and if they remained they would be paid for anything taken from them. As proof of this the peasant had brought from Visloúkhovo a hundred rubles in notes (he did not know that they were false) paid to him in advance for hay.

More important still, Alpátych learned that on the morning of the very day he gave the village Elder orders to collect carts to move the princess' luggage from Boguchárovo, there had been a village meeting at which it had been decided not to move but to wait. Yet there was no time to waste. On the fifteenth, the day of the old prince's death, the Marshal had insisted on Princess Mary's leaving at once, as it was becoming dangerous. He had told her that after the sixteenth he could not be responsible for what might happen. On the evening of the day the old prince died the Marshal went away, promising to return next day for the funeral. But this he was unable to do, for he received tidings that the French had unexpectedly advanced, and had barely time to remove his own family and valuables from his estate.

For some thirty years Boguchárovo had been managed by the village Elder, Dron, whom the old prince called by the diminutive "Drónushka."

Dron was one of those physically and mentally vigorous peasants who grow big beards as soon as they are of age and go on unchanged till they are sixty or seventy, without a gray hair or the loss of a tooth, as straight and strong at sixty as at thirty.

Soon after the migration to the "warm rivers," in which he had taken part like the rest, Dron was made village Elder and overseer of Boguchárovo, and had since filled that post irreproachably for twenty-three years. The peasants feared him more than they did their master. The masters, both the old prince and the young, and the steward respected him and jestingly called him "the Minister." During the whole time of his service Dron had never been drunk or ill, never after sleepless nights or the hardest tasks had he shown the least fatigue, and though he could not read he had never forgotten a single money account or the number of quarters of flour in any of the endless cartloads he sold for the prince, nor a single shock of the whole corn crop on any single acre of the Boguchárovo fields.

Alpátych, arriving from the devastated Bald Hills estate, sent for his Dron on the day of the prince's funeral and told him to have twelve horses got ready for the princess' carriages and eighteen carts for the things to be removed from Boguchárovo. Though the peasants paid quitrent, Alpátych thought no difficulty would be made about complying with this order, for there were two hundred and thirty households at work in Boguchárovo and the peasants were well to do. But on hearing the order Dron lowered his eyes and remained silent. Alpátych named certain peasants he knew, from whom he told him to take the carts.

Dron replied that the horses of these peasants were away carting. Alpátych named others, but they too, according to Dron, had no horses available: some horses were carting for the government, others were too weak, and others had died for want of fodder. It seemed that no horses could be had even for the carriages, much less for the carting.

Alpátych looked intently at Dron and frowned. Just as Dron was a model village Elder, so Alpátych had not managed the prince's estates for twenty years in vain. He was a model steward, possessing in the highest degree the faculty of divining the needs and instincts of those he dealt with. Having glanced at Dron he at once understood that his answers did not express his personal views but the general mood of the Boguchárovo commune, by which the Elder had already been carried away. But he also knew that Dron, who had acquired property and was hated by the commune, must be hesitating between the two camps: the masters' and the serfs'. He noticed this hesitation in Dron's look and therefore frowned and moved closer up to him.

"Now just listen, Drónushka," said he. "Don't talk nonsense to me. His excellency Prince Andrew himself gave me orders to move all the people away and not leave them with the enemy, and there is an order from the Tsar about it too. Anyone who stays is a traitor to the Tsar. Do you hear?"

"I hear," Dron answered without lifting his eyes.

Alpátych was not satisfied with this reply.

"Eh, Dron, it will turn out badly!" he said, shaking his head.

"The power is in your hands," Dron rejoined sadly.

"Eh, Dron, drop it!" Alpátych repeated, withdrawing his hand from his bosom and solemnly pointing to the floor at Dron's feet. "I can see through you and three yards into the ground under you," he continued, gazing at the floor in front of Dron.

Dron was disconcerted, glanced furtively at Alpátych and again lowered his eyes.

"You drop this nonsense and tell the people to get ready to leave their homes and go to Moscow and to get carts ready for tomorrow morning for the princess' things. And don't go to any meeting yourself, do you hear?"

Dron suddenly fell on his knees.

"YákovAlpátych, discharge me! Take the keys from me and discharge me, for Christ's sake!"

"Stop that!" cried Alpátych sternly. "I see through you and three yards under you," he repeated, knowing that his skill in beekeeping, his knowledge of the right time to sow the oats, and the fact that he had been able to retain the old prince's favor for twenty years had long since gained him the reputation of being a wizard, and that the power of seeing three yards under a man is considered an attribute of wizards.

Dron got up and was about to say something, but Alpátych interrupted him.

"What is it you have got into your heads, eh?... What are you thinking of, eh?"

"What am I to do with the people?" said Dron. "They're quite beside themselves; I have already told them..."

"'Told them,' I dare say!" said Alpátych. "Are they drinking?" he asked abruptly.

"Quite beside themselves, YákovAlpátych; they've fetched another barrel."

"Well, then, listen! I'll go to the police officer, and you tell them so, and that they must stop this and the carts must be got ready."

"I understand."

Alpátych did not insist further. He had managed people for a long time and knew that the chief way to make them obey is to show no suspicion that they can possibly disobey. Having wrung a submissive "I understand" from Dron, Alpátych contented himself with that, though he not only doubted but felt almost certain that without the help of troops the carts would not be forthcoming.

And so it was, for when evening came no carts had been provided. In the village, outside the drink shop, another meeting was being held, which decided that the horses should be driven out into the woods and the carts should not be provided. Without saying anything of this to the princess, Alpátych had his own belongings taken out of the carts which had arrived from Bald Hills and had those horses got ready for the princess' carriages. Meanwhile he went himself to the police authorities.

CHAPTER X

After her father's funeral Princess Mary shut herself up in her room and did not admit anyone. A maid came to the door to say that Alpátych was asking for orders about their departure. (This was before his talk with Dron.) Princess Mary raised herself on the sofa on which she had been lying and replied through the closed door that she did not mean to go away and begged to be left in peace.

The windows of the room in which she was lying looked westward. She lay on the sofa with her face to the wall, fingering the buttons of the leather cushion and seeing nothing but that cushion, and her confused thoughts were centered on one subject—the irrevocability of death and her own spiritual baseness, which she had not suspected, but which had shown itself during her father's illness. She wished to pray but did not dare to, dared not in her present state of mind address herself to God. She lay for a long time in that position.

The sun had reached the other side of the house, and its slanting rays shone into the open window, lighting up the room and part of the morocco cushion at which Princess Mary was looking. The flow of her thoughts suddenly stopped. Unconsciously she sat up, smoothed her hair, got up, and went to the window, involuntarily inhaling the freshness of the clear but windy evening.

"Yes, you can well enjoy the evening now! He is gone and no one will hinder you," she said to herself, and sinking into a chair she let her head fall on the window sill.

Someone spoke her name in a soft and tender voice from the garden and kissed her head. She looked up. It was Mademoiselle Bourienne in a black dress and weepers. She softly approached

Princess Mary, sighed, kissed her, and immediately began to cry. The princess looked up at her. All their former disharmony and her own jealousy recurred to her mind. But she remembered too how *he* had changed of late toward Mademoiselle Bourienne and could not bear to see her, thereby showing how unjust were the reproaches Princess Mary had mentally addressed to her. "Besides, is it for me, for me who desired his death, to condemn anyone?" she thought.

Princess Mary vividly pictured to herself the position of Mademoiselle Bourienne, whom she had of late kept at a distance, but who yet was dependent on her and living in her house. She felt sorry for her and held out her hand with a glance of gentle inquiry. Mademoiselle Bourienne at once began crying again and kissed that hand, speaking of the princess' sorrow and making herself a partner in it. She said her only consolation was the fact that the princess allowed her to share her sorrow, that all the old misunderstandings should sink into nothing but this great grief; that she felt herself blameless in regard to everyone, and that *he*, from above, saw her affection and gratitude. The princess heard her, not heeding her words but occasionally looking up at her and listening to the sound of her voice.

"Your position is doubly terrible, dear princess," said Mademoiselle Bourienne after a pause. "I understand that you could not, and cannot, think of yourself, but with my love for you I must do so.... Has Alpátych been to you? Has he spoken to you of going away?" she asked.

Princess Mary did not answer. She did not understand who was to go or where to. "Is it possible to plan or think of anything now? Is it not all the same?" she thought, and did not reply.

"You know, *chère Marie*," said Mademoiselle Bourienne, "that we are in danger—are surrounded by the French. It would be dangerous to move now. If we go we are almost sure to be taken prisoners, and God knows..."

Princess Mary looked at her companion without understanding what she was talking about.

"Oh, if anyone knew how little anything matters to me now," she said. "Of course I would on no account wish to go away from him.... Alpátych did say something about going.... Speak to him; I can do nothing, nothing, and don't want to...."

"I've spoken to him. He hopes we should be in time to get away tomorrow, but I think it would now be better to stay here," said Mademoiselle Bourienne. "Because, you will agree, *chère Marie*, to fall into the hands of the soldiers or of riotous peasants would be terrible."

Mademoiselle Bourienne took from her reticule a proclamation (not printed on ordinary Russian paper) of General Rameau's, telling people not to leave their homes and that the French authorities would afford them proper protection. She handed this to the princess.

"I think it would be best to appeal to that general," she continued, "and I am sure that all due respect would be shown you."

Princess Mary read the paper, and her face began to quiver with stifled sobs.

"From whom did you get this?" she asked.

"They probably recognized that I am French, by my name," replied Mademoiselle Bourienne blushing.

Princess Mary, with the paper in her hand, rose from the window and with a pale face went out of the room and into what had been Prince Andrew's study.

"Dunyásha, send Alpátych, or Drónushka, or somebody to me!" she said, "and tell Mademoiselle Bourienne not to come to me," she added, hearing Mademoiselle Bourienne's voice. "We must go at once, at once!" she said, appalled at the thought of being left in the hands of the French.

"If Prince Andrew heard that I was in the power of the French! That I, the daughter of Prince Nicholas Bolkónski, asked General Rameau for protection and accepted his favor!" This idea horrified her, made her shudder, blush, and feel such a rush of anger and pride as she had never experienced before. All that was distressing, and especially all that was humiliating, in her position rose vividly to her mind. "They, the French, would settle in this house: M. le Général Rameau would occupy Prince Andrew's study and amuse himself by looking through and reading his letters and papers. Mademoiselle Bourienne would do the honors of Boguchárovo for him. I should be given a small room as a favor, the soldiers would violate my father's newly dug grave to steal his crosses and stars, they would tell me of their victories over the Russians, and would pretend to sympathize with my sorrow..." thought Princess Mary, not thinking her own thoughts but feeling bound to think like her father and her brother. For herself she did not care where she remained or what happened to her, but she felt herself the representative of her dead father and of Prince Andrew. Involuntarily she thought their thoughts and felt their feelings. What they would have said and what they would have done she felt bound to say and do. She went into Prince Andrew's study, trying to enter completely into his ideas, and considered her position.

The demands of life, which had seemed to her annihilated by her father's death, all at once rose before her with a new, previously unknown force and took possession of her.

Agitated and flushed she paced the room, sending now for Michael Ivánovich and now for Tíkhon or Dron. Dunyásha, the nurse, and the other maids could not say in how far Mademoiselle Bourienne's statement was correct. Alpátych was not at home, he had gone to the police. Neither could the architect Michael Ivánovich, who on being sent for came in with sleepy eyes, tell Princess Mary anything. With just the same smile of agreement with which for fifteen years he had been accustomed to answer the old prince without expressing views of his own, he now replied to Princess Mary, so that nothing definite could be got from his answers. The old valet Tíkhon, with sunken, emaciated face that bore the stamp of inconsolable grief, replied: "Yes, Princess" to all Princess Mary's questions and hardly refrained from sobbing as he looked at her.

At length Dron, the village Elder, entered the room and with a deep bow to Princess Mary came to a halt by the doorpost.

Princess Mary walked up and down the room and stopped in front of him.

"Drónushka," she said, regarding as a sure friend this Drónushka who always used to bring a special kind of gingerbread from his visit to the fair at Vyázma every year and smilingly offer it to her, "Drónushka, now since our misfortune..." she began, but could not go on.

"We are all in God's hands," said he, with a sigh.

They were silent for a while.

"Drónushka, Alpátych has gone off somewhere and I have no one to turn to. Is it true, as they tell me, that I can't even go away?"

"Why shouldn't you go away, your excellency? You can go," said Dron.

"I was told it would be dangerous because of the enemy. Dear friend, I can do nothing. I understand nothing. I have nobody! I want to go away tonight or early tomorrow morning."

Dron paused. He looked askance at Princess Mary and said: "There are no horses; I told YákovAlpátych so."

"Why are there none?" asked the princess.

"It's all God's scourge," said Dron. "What horses we had have been taken for the army or have died—this is such a year! It's not a case of feeding horses—we may die of hunger ourselves! As it is, some go three days without eating. We've nothing, we've been ruined."

Princess Mary listened attentively to what he told her.

"The peasants are ruined? They have no bread?" she asked.

"They're dying of hunger," said Dron. "It's not a case of carting."

"But why didn't you tell me, Drónushka? Isn't it possible to help them? I'll do all I can...."

To Princess Mary it was strange that now, at a moment when such sorrow was filling her soul, there could be rich people and poor, and the rich could refrain from helping the poor. She had heard vaguely that there was such a thing as "landlord's corn" which was sometimes given to the peasants. She also knew that neither her father nor her brother would refuse to help the peasants in need, she only feared to make some mistake in speaking about the distribution of the grain she wished to give. She was glad such cares presented themselves, enabling her without scruple to forget her own grief. She began asking Dron about the peasants' needs and what there was in Boguchárovo that belonged to the landlord.

"But we have grain belonging to my brother?" she said.

"The landlord's grain is all safe," replied Dron proudly. "Our prince did not order it to be sold."

"Give it to the peasants, let them have all they need; I give you leave in my brother's name," said she.

Dron made no answer but sighed deeply.

"Give them that corn if there is enough of it. Distribute it all. I give this order in my brother's name; and tell them that what is ours is theirs. We do not grudge them anything. Tell them so."

Dron looked intently at the princess while she was speaking.

"Discharge me, little mother, for God's sake! Order the keys to be taken from me," said he. "I have served twenty-three years and have done no wrong. Discharge me, for God's sake!"

Princess Mary did not understand what he wanted of her or why he was asking to be discharged. She replied that she had never doubted his devotion and that she was ready to do anything for him and for the peasants.

CHAPTER XI

An hour later Dunyásha came to tell the princess that Dron had come, and all the peasants had assembled at the barn by the princess' order and wished to have word with their mistress.

"But I never told them to come," said Princess Mary. "I only told Dron to let them have the grain."

"Only, for God's sake, Princess dear, have them sent away and don't go out to them. It's all a trick," said Dunyásha, "and when YákovAlpátych returns let us get away... and please don't..."

"What is a trick?" asked Princess Mary in surprise.

"I know it is, only listen to me for God's sake! Ask nurse too. They say they don't agree to leave Boguchárovo as you ordered."

"You're making some mistake. I never ordered them to go away," said Princess Mary. "Call Drónushka."

Dron came and confirmed Dunyásha's words; the peasants had come by the princess' order.

"But I never sent for them," declared the princess. "You must have given my message wrong. I only said that you were to give them the grain."

Dron only sighed in reply.

"If you order it they will go away," said he.

"No, no. I'll go out to them," said Princess Mary, and in spite of the nurse's and Dunyásha's protests she went out into the porch; Dron, Dunyásha, the nurse, and Michael Ivánovich following her.

"They probably think I am offering them the grain to bribe them to remain here, while I myself go away leaving them to the mercy of the French," thought Princess Mary. "I will offer them monthly rations and housing at our Moscow estate. I am sure Andrew would do even more in my place," she thought as she went out in the twilight toward the crowd standing on the pasture by the barn.

The men crowded closer together, stirred, and rapidly took off their hats. Princess Mary lowered her eyes and, tripping over her skirt, came close up to them. So many different eyes, old and young, were fixed on her, and there were so many different faces, that she could not distinguish any of them and, feeling that she must speak to them all at once, did not know how to do it. But again the sense that she represented her father and her brother gave her courage, and she boldly began her speech.

"I am very glad you have come," she said without raising her eyes, and feeling her heart beating quickly and violently. "Drónushka tells me that the war has ruined you. That is our common misfortune, and I shall grudge nothing to help you. I am myself going away because it is dangerous here... the enemy is near... because... I am giving you everything, my friends, and I beg you to take everything, all our grain, so that you may not suffer want! And if you have been told that I am giving you the grain to keep you here—that is not true. On the contrary, I ask you to go with all your belongings to our estate near Moscow, and I promise you I will see to it that there you shall want for nothing. You shall be given food and lodging."

The princess stopped. Sighs were the only sound heard in the crowd.

"I am not doing this on my own account," she continued, "I do it in the name of my dead father, who was a good master to you, and of my brother and his son."

Again she paused. No one broke the silence.

"Ours is a common misfortune and we will share it together. All that is mine is yours," she concluded, scanning the faces before her.

All eyes were gazing at her with one and the same expression. She could not fathom whether it was curiosity, devotion, gratitude, or apprehension and distrust—but the expression on all the faces was identical.

"We are all very thankful for your bounty, but it won't do for us to take the landlord's grain," said a voice at the back of the crowd.

"But why not?" asked the princess.

No one replied and Princess Mary, looking round at the crowd, found that every eye she met now was immediately dropped.

"But why don't you want to take it?" she asked again.

No one answered.

The silence began to oppress the princess and she tried to catch someone's eye.

"Why don't you speak?" she inquired of a very old man who stood just in front of her leaning on his stick. "If you think something more is wanted, tell me! I will do anything," said she, catching his eye.

But as if this angered him, he bent his head quite low and muttered:

"Why should we agree? We don't want the grain."

"Why should we give up everything? We don't agree. Don't agree.... We are sorry for you, but we're not willing. Go away yourself, alone..." came from various sides of the crowd.

And again all the faces in that crowd bore an identical expression, though now it was certainly not an expression of curiosity or gratitude, but of angry resolve.

"But you can't have understood me," said Princess Mary with a sad smile. "Why don't you want to go? I promise to house and feed you, while here the enemy would ruin you...."

But her voice was drowned by the voices of the crowd.

"We're not willing. Let them ruin us! We won't take your grain. We don't agree."

Again Princess Mary tried to catch someone's eye, but not a single eye in the crowd was turned to her; evidently they were all trying to avoid her look. She felt strange and awkward.

"Oh yes, an artful tale! Follow her into slavery! Pull down your houses and go into bondage! I dare say! 'I'll give you grain, indeed!' she says," voices in the crowd were heard saying.

With drooping head Princess Mary left the crowd and went back to the house. Having repeated her order to Dron to have horses ready for her departure next morning, she went to her room and remained alone with her own thoughts.

CHAPTER XII

For a long time that night Princess Mary sat by the open window of her room hearing the sound of the peasants' voices that reached her from the village, but it was not of them she was thinking. She felt that she could not understand them however much she might think about them. She thought only of one thing, her sorrow, which, after the break caused by cares for the present, seemed already to belong to the past. Now she could remember it and weep or pray.

After sunset the wind had dropped. The night was calm and fresh. Toward midnight the voices began to subside, a cock crowed, the full moon began to show from behind the lime trees, a fresh white dewy mist began to rise, and stillness reigned over the village and the house.

Pictures of the near past—her father's illness and last moments— rose one after another to her memory. With mournful pleasure she now lingered over these images, repelling with horror only the last one, the picture of his death, which she felt she could not contemplate even in imagination at this still and mystic hour of night. And these pictures presented themselves to her so clearly and in such detail that they seemed now present, now past, and now future.

She vividly recalled the moment when he had his first stroke and was being dragged along by his armpits through the garden at Bald Hills, muttering something with his helpless tongue, twitching his gray eyebrows and looking uneasily and timidly at her.

"Even then he wanted to tell me what he told me the day he died," she thought. "He had always thought what he said then." And she recalled in all its detail the night at Bald Hills before he had the last stroke, when with a foreboding of disaster she had remained at home against his will. She had not slept and had stolen downstairs on tiptoe, and going to the door of the conservatory where he slept that night had listened at the door. In a suffering and weary voice he was saying something to Tíkhon, speaking of the Crimea and its warm nights and of the Empress. Evidently he had wanted to talk. "And why didn't he call me? Why didn't he let me be there instead of Tíkhon?" Princess Mary had thought and thought again now. "Now he will never tell anyone what he had in his soul. Never will that moment return for him or for me when he might have said all he longed to say, and not Tíkhon but I might have heard and understood him. Why didn't I enter the room?" she thought. "Perhaps he would then have said to me what he said the day he died. While talking to Tíkhon he asked about me twice. He wanted to see me, and I was standing close by, outside the door. It was sad and painful for him to talk to Tíkhon who did not understand him. I remember how he began speaking to him about Lise as if she were alive—he had forgotten she was dead—and Tíkhon reminded him that she was no more, and he shouted, 'Fool!' He was greatly depressed. From behind the door I heard how he lay down on his bed groaning and loudly exclaimed, 'My God!' Why didn't I go in then? What could he have done to me? What could I have lost? And perhaps he would then have been comforted and would have said that word to me." And Princess Mary uttered aloud the caressing word he had said to her on the day of his death. "Dear-est!" she repeated, and began sobbing, with tears that relieved her soul. She now saw his face before her. And not the face she had known ever since she could remember and had always seen at a distance, but the timid, feeble face she had seen for the first time quite closely, with all its wrinkles and details, when she stooped near to his mouth to catch what he said.

"Dear-est!" she repeated again.

"What was he thinking when he uttered that word? What is he thinking now?" This question suddenly presented itself to her, and in answer she saw him before her with the expression that was on his face as he lay in his coffin with his chin bound up with a white handkerchief. And the horror that had seized her when she touched him and convinced herself that *that* was not *he*, but something mysterious and horrible, seized her again. She tried to think of something else and to pray, but could do neither. With wide-open eyes she gazed at the moonlight and the shadows, expecting every moment to see his dead face, and she felt that the silence brooding over the house and within it held her fast.

"Dunyásha," she whispered. "Dunyásha!" she screamed wildly, and tearing herself out of this silence she ran to the servants' quarters to meet her old nurse and the maidservants who came running toward her.

CHAPTER XIII

O n the seventeenth of August Rostóv and Ilyín, accompanied by Lavrúshka who had just returned from captivity and by an hussar orderly, left their quarters at Yankóvo, ten miles from Boguchárovo, and went for a ride—to try a new horse Ilyín had bought and to find out whether there was any hay to be had in the villages.

For the last three days Boguchárovo had lain between the two hostile armies, so that it was as easy for the Russian rearguard to get to it as for the French vanguard; Rostóv, as a careful squadron commander, wished to take such provisions as remained at Boguchárovo before the French could get them.

Rostóv and Ilyín were in the merriest of moods. On the way to Boguchárovo, a princely estate with a dwelling house and farm where they hoped to find many domestic serfs and pretty girls, they questioned Lavrúshka about Napoleon and laughed at his stories, and raced one another to try Ilyín's horse.

Rostóv had no idea that the village he was entering was the property of that very Bolkónski who had been engaged to his sister.

Rostóv and Ilyín gave rein to their horses for a last race along the incline before reaching Boguchárovo, and Rostóv, outstripping Ilyín, was the first to gallop into the village street.

"You're first!" cried Ilyín, flushed.

"Yes, always first both on the grassland and here," answered Rostóv, stroking his heated Donéts horse.

"And I'd have won on my Frenchy, your excellency," said Lavrúshka from behind, alluding to his shabby cart horse, "only I didn't wish to mortify you."

They rode at a footpace to the barn, where a large crowd of peasants was standing.

Some of the men bared their heads, others stared at the new arrivals without doffing their caps. Two tall old peasants with wrinkled faces and scanty beards emerged from the tavern, smiling, staggering, and singing some incoherent song, and approached the officers.

"Fine fellows!" said Rostóv laughing. "Is there any hay here?"

"And how like one another," said Ilyín.

"A mo-o-st me-r-r-y co-o-m-pa...!" sang one of the peasants with a blissful smile.

One of the men came out of the crowd and went up to Rostóv.

"Who do you belong to?" he asked.

"The French," replied Ilyín jestingly, "and here is Napoleon himself"—and he pointed to Lavrúshka.

"Then you are Russians?" the peasant asked again.

"And is there a large force of you here?" said another, a short man, coming up.

"Very large," answered Rostóv. "But why have you collected here?" he added. "Is it a holiday?"

"The old men have met to talk over the business of the commune," replied the peasant, moving away.

At that moment, on the road leading from the big house, two women and a man in a white hat were seen coming toward the officers.

"The one in pink is mine, so keep off!" said Ilyín on seeing Dunyásha running resolutely toward him.

"She'll be ours!" said Lavrúshka to Ilyín, winking.

"What do you want, my pretty?" said Ilyín with a smile.

"The princess ordered me to ask your regiment and your name."

"This is Count Rostóv, squadron commander, and I am your humble servant."

"Co-o-om-pa-ny!" roared the tipsy peasant with a beatific smile as he looked at Ilyín talking to the girl. Following Dunyásha, Alpátych advanced to Rostóv, having bared his head while still at a distance.

"May I make bold to trouble your honor?" said he respectfully, but with a shade of contempt for the youthfulness of this officer and with a hand thrust into his bosom. "My mistress, daughter of General in Chief Prince Nicholas Bolkónski who died on the fifteenth of this month, finding herself in difficulties owing to the boorishness of these people"—he pointed to the peasants—"asks you to come up to the house.... Won't you, please, ride on a little farther," said Alpátych with a melancholy smile, "as it is not convenient in the presence of...?" He pointed to the two peasants who kept as close to him as horseflies to a horse.

"Ah!... Alpátych... Ah, YákovAlpátych... Grand! Forgive us for Christ's sake, eh?" said the peasants, smiling joyfully at him.

Rostóv looked at the tipsy peasants and smiled.

"Or perhaps they amuse your honor?" remarked Alpátych with a staid air, as he pointed at the old men with his free hand.

"No, there's not much to be amused at here," said Rostóv, and rode on a little way. "What's the matter?" he asked.

"I make bold to inform your honor that the rude peasants here don't wish to let the mistress leave the estate, and threaten to unharness her horses, so that though everything has been packed up since morning, her excellency cannot get away."

"Impossible!" exclaimed Rostóv.

"I have the honor to report to you the actual truth," said Alpátych.

Rostóv dismounted, gave his horse to the orderly, and followed Alpátych to the house, questioning him as to the state of affairs. It appeared that the princess' offer of corn to the peasants the previous day, and her talk with Dron and at the meeting, had actually had so bad an effect that Dron had finally given up the keys and joined the peasants and had not appeared when Alpátych sent for him; and that in the morning when the princess gave orders to harness for her journey, the peasants had come in a large crowd to the barn and sent word that they would not let her leave the village: that there was an order not to move, and that they would unharness the horses. Alpátych had gone out to admonish them, but was told (it was chiefly Karp who did the talking, Dron not showing himself in the crowd) that they could not let the princess go, that there was an order to the contrary, but that if she stayed they would serve her as before and obey her in everything.

At the moment when Rostóv and Ilyín were galloping along the road, Princess Mary, despite the dissuasions of Alpátych, her nurse, and the maids, had given orders to harness and intended to start, but when the cavalrymen were espied they were taken for Frenchmen, the coachman ran away, and the women in the house began to wail.

"Father! Benefactor! God has sent you!" exclaimed deeply moved voices as Rostóv passed through the anteroom.

Princess Mary was sitting helpless and bewildered in the large sitting room, when Rostóv was shown in. She could not grasp who he was and why he had come, or what was happening to her. When she saw his Russian face, and by his walk and the first words he uttered recognized him as a man of her own class, she glanced at him with her deep radiant look and began speaking in a voice that faltered and trembled with emotion. This meeting immediately struck Rostóv as a romantic event. "A helpless girl overwhelmed with grief, left to the mercy of coarse, rioting peasants! And what a strange fate sent me here! What gentleness and nobility there are in her features and expression!" thought he as he looked at her and listened to her timid story.

When she began to tell him that all this had happened the day after her father's funeral, her voice trembled. She turned away, and then, as if fearing he might take her words as meant to move him to pity, looked at him with an apprehensive glance of inquiry. There were tears in Rostóv's eyes. Princess Mary noticed this and glanced gratefully at him with that radiant look which caused the plainness of her face to be forgotten.

"I cannot express, Princess, how glad I am that I happened to ride here and am able to show my readiness to serve you," said Rostóv, rising. "Go when you please, and I give you my word of honor that no one shall dare to cause you annoyance if only you will allow me to act as your escort." And bowing respectfully, as if to a lady of royal blood, he moved toward the door.

Rostóv's deferential tone seemed to indicate that though he would consider himself happy to be acquainted with her, he did not wish to take advantage of her misfortunes to intrude upon her.

Princess Mary understood this and appreciated his delicacy.

"I am very, very grateful to you," she said in French, "but I hope it was all a misunderstanding and that no one is to blame for it." She suddenly began to cry.

"Excuse me!" she said.

Rostóv, knitting his brows, left the room with another low bow.

CHAPTER XIV

"Well, is she pretty? Ah, friend—my pink one is delicious; her name is Dunyásha...."

But on glancing at Rostóv's face Ilyín stopped short. He saw that his hero and commander was following quite a different train of thought.

Rostóv glanced angrily at Ilyín and without replying strode off with rapid steps to the village.

"I'll show them; I'll give it to them, the brigands!" said he to himself.

Alpátych at a gliding trot, only just managing not to run, kept up with him with difficulty.

"What decision have you been pleased to come to?" said he.

Rostóv stopped and, clenching his fists, suddenly and sternly turned on Alpátych.

"Decision? What decision? Old dotard!..." cried he. "What have you been about? Eh? The peasants are rioting, and you can't manage them? You're a traitor yourself! I know you. I'll flay you all alive!..." And as if afraid of wasting his store of anger, he left Alpátych and went rapidly forward. Alpátych, mastering his offended feelings, kept pace with Rostóv at a gliding gait and continued to impart his views. He said the peasants were obdurate and that at the present moment it would be imprudent to "overresist" them without an armed force, and would it not be better first to send for the military?

"I'll give them armed force... I'll 'overresist' them!" uttered Rostóv meaninglessly, breathless with irrational animal fury and the need to vent it.

Without considering what he would do he moved unconciously with quick, resolute steps toward the crowd. And the nearer he drew to it the more Alpátych felt that this unreasonable action might produce good results. The peasants in the crowd were similarly impressed when they saw Rostóv's rapid, firm steps and resolute, frowning face.

After the hussars had come to the village and Rostóv had gone to see the princess, a certain confusion and dissension had arisen among the crowd. Some of the peasants said that these new arrivals were Russians and might take it amiss that the mistress was being detained. Dron was of this opinion, but as soon as he expressed it Karp and others attacked their ex-Elder.

"How many years have you been fattening on the commune?" Karp shouted at him. "It's all one to you! You'll dig up your pot of money and take it away with you.... What does it matter to you whether our homes are ruined or not?"

"We've been told to keep order, and that no one is to leave their homes or take away a single grain, and that's all about it!" cried another.

"It was your son's turn to be conscripted, but no fear! You begrudged your lump of a son," a little old man suddenly began attacking Dron—"and so they took my Vánka to be shaved for a soldier! But we all have to die."

"To be sure, we all have to die. I'm not against the commune," said Dron.

"That's it—not against it! You've filled your belly...."

The two tall peasants had their say. As soon as Rostóv, followed by Ilyín, Lavrúshka, and Alpátych, came up to the crowd, Karp, thrusting his fingers into his belt and smiling a little, walked to the front. Dron on the contrary retired to the rear and the crowd drew closer together.

"Who is your Elder here? Hey?" shouted Rostóv, coming up to the crowd with quick steps.

"The Elder? What do you want with him?..." asked Karp.

But before the words were well out of his mouth, his cap flew off and a fierce blow jerked his head to one side.

"Caps off, traitors!" shouted Rostóv in a wrathful voice. "Where's the Elder?" he cried furiously.

"The Elder.... He wants the Elder!... DronZakhárych, you!" meek and flustered voices here and there were heard calling and caps began to come off their heads.

"We don't riot, we're following the orders," declared Karp, and at that moment several voices began speaking together.

"It's as the old men have decided—there's too many of you giving orders."

"Arguing? Mutiny!... Brigands! Traitors!" cried Rostóv unmeaningly in a voice not his own, gripping Karp by the collar. "Bind him, bind him!" he shouted, though there was no one to bind him but Lavrúshka and Alpátych.

Lavrúshka, however, ran up to Karp and seized him by the arms from behind.

"Shall I call up our men from beyond the hill?" he called out.

Alpátych turned to the peasants and ordered two of them by name to come and bind Karp. The men obediently came out of the crowd and began taking off their belts.

"Where's the Elder?" demanded Rostóv in a loud voice.

With a pale and frowning face Dron stepped out of the crowd.

"Are you the Elder? Bind him, Lavrúshka!" shouted Rostóv, as if that order, too, could not possibly meet with any opposition.

And in fact two more peasants began binding Dron, who took off his own belt and handed it to them, as if to aid them.

"And you all listen to me!" said Rostóv to the peasants. "Be off to your houses at once, and don't let one of your voices be heard!"

"Why, we've not done any harm! We did it just out of foolishness. It's all nonsense.... I said then that it was not in order," voices were heard bickering with one another.

"There! What did I say?" said Alpátych, coming into his own again. "It's wrong, lads!"

"All our stupidity, YákovAlpátych," came the answers, and the crowd began at once to disperse through the village.

The two bound men were led off to the master's house. The two drunken peasants followed them.

"Aye, when I look at you!..." said one of them to Karp.

"How can one talk to the masters like that? What were you thinking of, you fool?" added the other—"A real fool!"

Two hours later the carts were standing in the courtyard of the Boguchárovo house. The peasants were briskly carrying out the proprietor's goods and packing them on the carts, and Dron, liberated at Princess Mary's wish from the cupboard where he had been confined, was standing in the yard directing the men.

"Don't put it in so carelessly," said one of the peasants, a man with a round smiling face, taking a casket from a housemaid. "You know it has cost money! How can you chuck it in like that or shove it under the cord where it'll get rubbed? I don't like that way of doing things. Let it all be done properly, according to rule. Look here, put it under the bast matting and cover it with hay—that's the way!"

"Eh, books, books!" said another peasant, bringing out Prince Andrew's library cupboards. "Don't catch up against it! It's heavy, lads—solid books."

"Yes, they worked all day and didn't play!" remarked the tall, round-faced peasant gravely, pointing with a significant wink at the dictionaries that were on the top.

Unwilling to obtrude himself on the princess, Rostóv did not go back to the house but remained in the village awaiting her departure. When her carriage drove out of the house, he mounted and accompanied her eight miles from Boguchárovo to where the road was occupied by our troops. At the inn at Yankóvo he respectfully took leave of her, for the first time permitting himself to kiss her hand.

"How can you speak so!" he blushingly replied to Princess Mary's expressions of gratitude for her deliverance, as she termed what had occurred. "Any police officer would have done as much! If we had had only peasants to fight, we should not have let the enemy come so far," said he with a sense of shame and wishing to change the subject. "I am only happy to have had the opportunity of making your acquaintance.

Good-by, Princess. I wish you happiness and consolation and hope to meet you again in happier circumstances. If you don't want to make me blush, please don't thank me!"

But the princess, if she did not again thank him in words, thanked him with the whole expression of her face, radiant with gratitude and tenderness. She could not believe that there was nothing to thank him for. On the contrary, it seemed to her certain that had he not been there she would have perished at the hands of the mutineers and of the French, and that he had exposed himself to terrible and obvious danger to save her, and even more certain was it that he was a man of lofty and noble soul, able to understand her position and her sorrow. His kind, honest eyes, with the tears rising in them when she herself had begun to cry as she spoke of her loss, did not leave her memory.

When she had taken leave of him and remained alone she suddenly felt her eyes filling with tears, and then not for the first time the strange question presented itself to her: did she love him?

On the rest of the way to Moscow, though the princess' position was not a cheerful one, Dunyásha, who went with her in the carriage, more than once noticed that her mistress leaned out of the window and smiled at something with an expression of mingled joy and sorrow.

"Well, supposing I do love him?" thought Princess Mary.

Ashamed as she was of acknowledging to herself that she had fallen in love with a man who would perhaps never love her, she comforted herself with the thought that no one would ever know it and that she would not be to blame if, without ever speaking of it to anyone, she continued to the end of her life to love the man with whom she had fallen in love for the first and last time in her life.

Sometimes when she recalled his looks, his sympathy, and his words, happiness did not appear impossible to her. It was at those moments that Dunyásha noticed her smiling as she looked out of the carriage window.

"Was it not fate that brought him to Boguchárovo, and at that very moment?" thought Princess Mary. "And that caused his sister to refuse my brother?" And in all this Princess Mary saw the hand of Providence.

The impression the princess made on Rostóv was a very agreeable one. To remember her gave him pleasure, and when his comrades, hearing of his adventure at Boguchárovo, rallied him on having gone to look for hay and having picked up one of the wealthiest heiresses in Russia, he grew angry. It made him angry just because the idea of marrying the gentle Princess Mary, who was attractive to him and had an enormous fortune, had against his will more than once entered his head. For himself personally Nicholas could not wish for a better wife: by marrying her he would make the countess his mother happy, would be able to put his father's affairs in order, and would even—he felt it—ensure Princess Mary's happiness.

But Sónya? And his plighted word? That was why Rostóv grew angry when he was rallied about Princess Bolkónskaya.

CHAPTER XV

O n receiving command of the armies Kutúzov remembered Prince Andrew and sent an order for him to report at headquarters.

Prince Andrew arrived at Tsárevo-Zaymíshche on the very day and at the very hour that Kutúzov was reviewing the troops for the first time. He stopped in the village at the priest's house in front of which stood the commander in chief's carriage, and he sat down on the bench at the gate awaiting his Serene Highness, as everyone now called Kutúzov. From the field beyond the village came now sounds of regimental music and now the roar of many voices shouting "Hurrah!" to the new commander in chief. Two orderlies, a courier and a major-domo, stood near by, some ten paces from Prince Andrew, availing themselves of Kutúzov's absence and of the fine weather. A short, swarthy lieutenant colonel of hussars with thick mustaches and whiskers rode up to the gate and, glancing at Prince Andrew, inquired whether his Serene Highness was putting up there and whether he would soon be back.

Prince Andrew replied that he was not on his Serene Highness' staff but was himself a new arrival. The lieutenant colonel turned to a smart orderly, who, with the peculiar contempt with which a commander in chief's orderly speaks to officers, replied:

"What? His Serene Highness? I expect he'll be here soon. What do you want?"

The lieutenant colonel of hussars smiled beneath his mustache at the orderly's tone, dismounted, gave his horse to a dispatch runner, and approached Bolkónski with a slight bow. Bolkónski made room for him on the bench and the lieutenant colonel sat down beside him.

"You're also waiting for the commander in chief?" said he. "They say he weceivesevewyone, thank God!... It's awful with those sausage eaters! Ermólov had weason to ask to be pwomoted to be a German! Now p'wapsWussians will get a look in. As it was, devil only knows what was happening. We kept wetweating and wetweating. Did you take part in the campaign?" he asked.

"I had the pleasure," replied Prince Andrew, "not only of taking part in the retreat but of losing in that retreat all I held dear—not to mention the estate and home of my birth—my father, who died of grief. I belong to the province of Smolénsk."

"Ah? You're PwinceBolkónski? Vewy glad to make your acquaintance! I'm Lieutenant Colonel Denísov, better known as 'Váska,'" said Denísov, pressing Prince Andrew's hand and looking into his face with a particularly kindly attention. "Yes, I heard," said he sympathetically, and after a short pause added: "Yes, it's Scythian warfare. It's all vewy well—only not for those who get it in the neck. So you are PwinceAndwewBolkónski?" He swayed his head. "Vewy pleased, Pwince, to make your acquaintance!" he repeated again, smiling sadly, and he again pressed Prince Andrew's hand.

Prince Andrew knew Denísov from what Natásha had told him of her first suitor. This memory carried him sadly and sweetly back to those painful feelings of which he had not thought lately, but which still found place in his soul. Of late he had received so many new and very serious impressions—such as the retreat from Smolénsk, his visit to Bald Hills, and the recent news of his father's death—and had experienced so many emotions, that for a long time past those memories had not entered his mind, and now that they did, they did not act on him with nearly their former strength. For Denísov, too, the memories awakened by the name of Bolkónski belonged to a distant, romantic past, when after supper and after Natásha's singing he had proposed to a little girl of fifteen without realizing what he was doing. He smiled at the recollection of that time and of his love for Natásha, and passed at once to what now interested him passionately and exclusively. This was a plan of campaign he had devised while serving at the outposts during the retreat. He had proposed that plan to Barclay de Tolly and now wished to propose it to Kutúzov. The plan was based on the fact that the French line of operation was too extended, and it proposed that instead of, or concurrently with, action on the front to bar the advance of the French, we should attack their line of communication. He began explaining his plan to Prince Andrew.

"They can't hold all that line. It's impossible. I will undertake to bweakthwough. Give me five hundwed men and I will bweak the line, that's certain! There's only one way—guewilla warfare!"

Denísov rose and began gesticulating as he explained his plan to Bolkónski. In the midst of his explanation shouts were heard from the army, growing more incoherent and more diffused, mingling with music and songs and coming from the field where the review was held. Sounds of hoofs and shouts were nearing the village.

"He's coming! He's coming!" shouted a Cossack standing at the gate.

Bolkónski and Denísov moved to the gate, at which a knot of soldiers (a guard of honor) was standing, and they saw Kutúzov coming down the street mounted on a rather small sorrel horse. A huge suite of generals rode behind him. Barclay was riding almost beside him, and a crowd of officers ran after and around them shouting, "Hurrah!"

His adjutants galloped into the yard before him. Kutúzov was impatiently urging on his horse, which ambled smoothly under his weight, and he raised his hand to his white Horse Guard's cap with a red band and no peak, nodding his head continually. When he came up to the guard of honor, a fine set of Grenadiers mostly wearing decorations, who were giving him the salute, he looked at them silently and attentively for nearly a minute with the steady gaze of a commander and then turned to the crowd of generals and officers surrounding him. Suddenly his face assumed a subtle expression, he shrugged his shoulders with an air of perplexity.

"And with such fine fellows to retreat and retreat! Well, good-by, General," he added, and rode into the yard past Prince Andrew and Denísov.

"Hurrah! hurrah! hurrah!" shouted those behind him.

Since Prince Andrew had last seen him Kutúzov had grown still more corpulent, flaccid, and fat. But the bleached eyeball, the scar, and the familiar weariness of his expression were still the same. He was wearing the white Horse Guard's cap and a military overcoat with a whip hanging over his shoulder by a thin strap. He sat heavily and swayed limply on his brisk little horse.

"Whew... whew... whew!" he whistled just audibly as he rode into the yard. His face expressed the relief of relaxed strain felt by a man who means to rest after a ceremony. He drew his left foot out of the stirrup and, lurching with his whole body and puckering his face with the effort, raised it with difficulty onto the saddle, leaned on his knee, groaned, and slipped down into the arms of the Cossacks and adjutants who stood ready to assist him.

He pulled himself together, looked round, screwing up his eyes, glanced at Prince Andrew, and, evidently not recognizing him, moved with his waddling gait to the porch. "Whew... whew... whew!" he whistled, and again glanced at Prince Andrew. As often occurs with old men, it was only after some seconds that the impression produced by Prince Andrew's face linked itself up with Kutúzov's remembrance of his personality.

"Ah, how do you do, my dear prince? How do you do, my dear boy? Come along..." said he, glancing wearily round, and he stepped onto the porch which creaked under his weight.

He unbuttoned his coat and sat down on a bench in the porch.

"And how's your father?"

"I received news of his death, yesterday," replied Prince Andrew abruptly.

Kutúzov looked at him with eyes wide open with dismay and then took off his cap and crossed himself:

"May the kingdom of Heaven be his! God's will be done to us all!" He sighed deeply, his whole chest heaving, and was silent for a while. "I loved him and respected him, and sympathize with you with all my heart."

He embraced Prince Andrew, pressing him to his fat breast, and for some time did not let him go. When he released him Prince Andrew saw that Kutúzov's flabby lips were trembling and that tears were in his eyes. He sighed and pressed on the bench with both hands to raise himself.

"Come! Come with me, we'll have a talk," said he.

But at that moment Denísov, no more intimidated by his superiors than by the enemy, came with jingling spurs up the steps of the porch, despite the angry whispers of the adjutants who tried to stop him. Kutúzov, his hands still pressed on the seat, glanced at him glumly. Denísov, having given his name, announced that he had to communicate to his Serene Highness a matter of great importance for their country's welfare. Kutúzov looked wearily at him and, lifting his hands with a gesture of annoyance, folded them across his stomach, repeating the words: "For our country's welfare? Well, what is it? Speak!" Denísov blushed like a girl (it was strange to see the color rise in that shaggy, bibulous, time-worn face) and boldly began to expound his plan of cutting the enemy's lines of communication between Smolénsk and Vyázma. Denísov came from those parts and knew the country well. His plan seemed decidedly a good one, especially from the strength of conviction with which he spoke. Kutúzov looked down at his own legs, occasionally glancing at the door of the adjoining hut as if expecting something unpleasant to emerge from it. And from that hut, while Denísov was speaking, a general with a portfolio under his arm really did appear.

"What?" said Kutúzov, in the midst of Denísov's explanations, "are you ready so soon?"

"Ready, your Serene Highness," replied the general.

Kutúzov swayed his head, as much as to say: "How is one man to deal with it all?" and again listened to Denísov.

"I give my word of honor as a Wussian officer," said Denísov, "that I can bweak Napoleon's line of communication!"

"What relation are you to Intendant General KirílAndréevichDenísov?" asked Kutúzov, interrupting him.

"He is my uncle, your Sewene Highness."

"Ah, we were friends," said Kutúzov cheerfully. "All right, all right, friend, stay here at the staff and tomorrow we'll have a talk."

With a nod to Denísov he turned away and put out his hand for the papers Konovnítsyn had brought him.

"Would not your Serene Highness like to come inside?" said the general on duty in a discontented voice, "the plans must be examined and several papers have to be signed."

An adjutant came out and announced that everything was in readiness within. But Kutúzov evidently did not wish to enter that room till he was disengaged. He made a grimace....

"No, tell them to bring a small table out here, my dear boy. I'll look at them here," said he. "Don't go away," he added, turning to Prince Andrew, who remained in the porch and listened to the general's report.

While this was being given, Prince Andrew heard the whisper of a woman's voice and the rustle of a silk dress behind the door. Several times on glancing that way he noticed behind that door a plump, rosy, handsome woman in a pink dress with a lilac silk kerchief on her head, holding a dish and evidently awaiting the entrance of the commander in chief. Kutúzov's adjutant whispered to Prince Andrew that this was the wife of the priest whose home it was, and that she intended to offer his Serene Highness bread and salt. "Her husband has welcomed his Serene Highness with the cross at the church, and she intends to welcome him in the house.... She's very pretty," added the adjutant with a smile. At those words Kutúzov looked round. He was listening to the general's report—which consisted chiefly of a criticism of the position at Tsárevo-Zaymíshche—as he had listened to Denísov, and seven years previously had listened to the discussion at the Austerlitz council of war. He evidently listened only because he had ears which, though there was a piece of tow in one of them, could not help hearing; but it was evident that nothing the general could say would surprise or even interest him, that he knew all that would be said beforehand, and heard it all only because he had to, as one has to listen to the chanting of a service of prayer. All that Denísov had said was clever and to the point. What the general was saying was even more clever and to the point, but it was evident that Kutúzov despised knowledge and cleverness, and knew of something else that would decide the matter—something independent of cleverness and knowledge. Prince Andrew watched the commander in chief's face attentively, and the only expression he could see there was one of boredom, curiosity as to the meaning of the feminine whispering behind the door, and a desire to observe propriety. It was evident that Kutúzov despised cleverness and learning and even the patriotic feeling shown by Denísov, but despised them not because of his own intellect, feelings, or knowledge—he did not try to display any of these—but because of something else. He despised them because of his old age and experience of life. The only instruction Kutúzov gave of his own accord during that report referred to looting by the Russian troops. At the end of the report the general put before him for signature a paper relating to the recovery of payment from army commanders for green oats mown down by the soldiers, when landowners lodged petitions for compensation.

After hearing the matter, Kutúzov smacked his lips together and shook his head.

"Into the stove... into the fire with it! I tell you once for all, my dear fellow," said he, "into the fire with all such things! Let them cut the crops and burn wood to their hearts' content. I don't order it or allow it, but I don't exact compensation either. One can't get on without it. 'When wood is chopped the chips will fly.'" He looked at the paper again. "Oh, this German precision!" he muttered, shaking his head.

CHAPTER XVI

"**W**ell, that's all!" said Kutúzov as he signed the last of the documents, and rising heavily and smoothing out the folds in his fat white neck he moved toward the door with a more cheerful expression.

The priest's wife, flushing rosy red, caught up the dish she had after all not managed to present at the right moment, though she had so long been preparing for it, and with a low bow offered it to Kutúzov.

He screwed up his eyes, smiled, lifted her chin with his hand, and said:

"Ah, what a beauty! Thank you, sweetheart!"

He took some gold pieces from his trouser pocket and put them on the dish for her. "Well, my dear, and how are we getting on?" he asked, moving to the door of the room assigned to him. The priest's wife smiled, and with dimples in her rosy cheeks followed him into the room. The adjutant came out to the porch and asked Prince Andrew to lunch with him. Half an hour later Prince Andrew was again called to Kutúzov. He found him reclining in an armchair, still in the same unbuttoned overcoat. He had in his hand a French book which he closed as Prince Andrew entered, marking the place with a knife. Prince Andrew saw by the cover that it was *Les Chevaliers du Cygne* by Madame de Genlis.

"Well, sit down, sit down here. Let's have a talk," said Kutúzov. "It's sad, very sad. But remember, my dear fellow, that I am a father to you, a second father...."

Prince Andrew told Kutúzov all he knew of his father's death, and what he had seen at Bald Hills when he passed through it.

"What... what they have brought us to!" Kutúzov suddenly cried in an agitated voice, evidently picturing vividly to himself from Prince Andrew's story the condition Russia was in. "But give me time, give me time!" he said with a grim look, evidently not wishing to continue this agitating conversation, and added: "I sent for you to keep you with me."

"I thank your Serene Highness, but I fear I am no longer fit for the staff," replied Prince Andrew with a smile which Kutúzov noticed.

Kutúzov glanced inquiringly at him.

"But above all," added Prince Andrew, "I have grown used to my regiment, am fond of the officers, and I fancy the men also like me. I should be sorry to leave the regiment. If I decline the honor of being with you, believe me..."

A shrewd, kindly, yet subtly derisive expression lit up Kutúzov's podgy face. He cut Bolkónski short.

"I am sorry, for I need you. But you're right, you're right! It's not here that men are needed. Advisers are always plentiful, but men are not. The regiments would not be what they are if the would-be advisers served there as you do. I remember you at Austerlitz.... I remember, yes, I remember you with the standard!" said Kutúzov, and a flush of pleasure suffused Prince Andrew's face at this recollection.

Taking his hand and drawing him downwards, Kutúzov offered his cheek to be kissed, and again Prince Andrew noticed tears in the old man's eyes. Though Prince Andrew knew that Kutúzov's tears came easily, and that he was particularly tender to and considerate of him from a wish to show sympathy with his loss, yet this reminder of Austerlitz was both pleasant and flattering to him.

"Go your way and God be with you. I know your path is the path of honor!" He paused. "I missed you at Bucharest, but I needed someone to send." And changing the subject, Kutúzov began to speak of the Turkish war and the peace that had been concluded. "Yes, I have been much blamed," he said, "both for that war and the peace... but everything came at the right time. *Tout vient à point à celui qui saitattendre.* * And there were as many advisers there as here..." he went on, returning to the subject of "advisers" which evidently occupied him. "Ah, those advisers!" said he. "If we had listened to them all we should not have made peace with Turkey and should not have been through with that war. Everything in haste, but more haste, less speed. Kámenski would have been lost if he had not died. He stormed fortresses with thirty thousand men. It is not difficult to capture a fortress but it is difficult to win a campaign. For that, not storming and attacking but *patience and time* are wanted. Kámenski sent soldiers to Rustchuk, but I only employed these two things and took more fortresses than Kámenski and made them Turks eat horseflesh!" He swayed his head. "And the French shall too, believe me," he went on, growing warmer and beating his chest, "I'll make them eat horseflesh!" And tears again dimmed his eyes.

* "Everything comes in time to him who knows how to wait."

"But shan't we have to accept battle?" remarked Prince Andrew.

"We shall if everybody wants it; it can't be helped.... But believe me, my dear boy, there is nothing stronger than those two: *patience and time*, they will do it all. But the advisers *n'entendent pas de cetteoreille, voilà le mal.* * Some want a thing—others don't. What's one to do?" he asked, evidently expecting an answer. "Well, what do you want us to do?" he repeated and his eye shone with a deep, shrewd look. "I'll tell you what to do," he continued, as Prince Andrew still did not reply: "I will tell you what to do, and what I do. *Dans le doute, moncher,*" he paused, *"abstiens-toi"* *(2)—he articulated the French proverb deliberately.

* "Don't see it that way, that's the trouble."

* (2) "When in doubt, my dear fellow, do nothing."

"Well, good-by, my dear fellow; remember that with all my heart I share your sorrow, and that for you I am not a Serene Highness, nor a prince, nor a commander in chief, but a father! If you want anything come straight to me. Good-by, my dear boy."

Again he embraced and kissed Prince Andrew, but before the latter had left the room Kutúzov gave a sigh of relief and went on with his unfinished novel, *Les Chevaliers du Cygne* by Madame de Genlis.

Prince Andrew could not have explained how or why it was, but after that interview with Kutúzov he went back to his regiment reassured as to the general course of affairs and as to the man to whom it had been entrusted. The more he realized the absence of all personal motive in that old man—in whom there seemed to remain only the habit of passions, and in place of an intellect (grouping events and drawing conclusions) only the capacity calmly to contemplate the course of events—the more reassured he was that everything would be as it should. "He will not bring in any plan of his own. He will not devise or undertake anything," thought Prince Andrew, "but he will hear everything, remember everything, and put everything in its place. He will not hinder anything useful nor allow anything harmful. He understands that there is something stronger and more important than his own will—the inevitable course of events, and he can see them and grasp their significance, and seeing that significance can refrain from meddling and renounce his personal wish directed to something else. And above all," thought Prince Andrew, "one believes in him because he's Russian, despite the novel by Genlis and the French proverbs, and because his voice shook when he said: 'What they have brought us to!' and had a sob in it when he said he would 'make them eat horseflesh!'"

On such feelings, more or less dimly shared by all, the unanimity and general approval were founded with which, despite court influences, the popular choice of Kutúzov as commander in chief was received.

CHAPTER XVII

After the Emperor had left Moscow, life flowed on there in its usual course, and its course was so very usual that it was difficult to remember the recent days of patriotic elation and ardor, hard to believe that Russia was really in danger and that the members of the English Club were also sons of the Fatherland ready to sacrifice everything for it. The one thing that recalled the patriotic fervor everyone had displayed during the Emperor's stay was the call for contributions of men and money, a necessity that as soon as the promises had been made assumed a legal, official form and became unavoidable.

With the enemy's approach to Moscow, the Moscovites' view of their situation did not grow more serious but on the contrary became even more frivolous, as always happens with people who see a great danger approaching. At the approach of danger there are always two voices that speak with equal power in the human soul: one very reasonably tells a man to consider the nature of the danger and the means of escaping it; the other, still more reasonably, says that it is too depressing and painful to think of the danger, since it is not in man's power to foresee everything and avert the general course of events, and it is therefore better to disregard what is painful till it comes, and to think about what is pleasant. In solitude a man generally listens to the first voice, but in society to the second. So it was now with the inhabitants of Moscow. It was long since people had been as gay in Moscow as that year.

Rostopchín's broadsheets, headed by woodcuts of a drink shop, a potman, and a Moscow burgher called KarpúshkaChigírin, *"who—having been a militiaman and having had rather too much at the pub—heard that Napoleon wished to come to Moscow, grew angry, abused the French in very bad language, came out of the drink shop, and, under the sign of the eagle, began to address the assembled people,"* were read and discussed, together with the latest of VasíliLvóvichPúshkin's *bouts rimés.*

In the corner room at the Club, members gathered to read these broadsheets, and some liked the way Karpúshka jeered at the French, saying: *"They will swell up with Russian cabbage, burst with our buckwheat porridge, and choke themselves with cabbage soup. They are all dwarfs and one peasant woman will toss three of them with a hayfork."* Others did not like that tone and said it was stupid and vulgar. It was said that Rostopchín had expelled all Frenchmen and even all foreigners from Moscow, and that there had been some spies and agents of Napoleon among them; but this was told chiefly to introduce Rostopchín's witty remark on that occasion. The foreigners were deported to Nízhni by boat, and Rostopchín had said to them in French: *"Rentrezenvous-mêmes; entrez dans la barque, et n'enfaites pas une barque de Charon."* * There was talk of all the government offices having been already removed from Moscow, and to this Shinshín's witticism was added—that for that alone Moscow ought to be grateful to Napoleon. It was said that Mamónov's regiment would cost him eight hundred thousand rubles, and that Bezúkhov had spent even more on his, but that the best thing about Bezúkhov's action was that he himself was going to don a uniform and ride at the head of his regiment without charging anything for the show.

* "Think it over; get into the barque, and take care not to make it a barque of Charon."

"You don't spare anyone," said Julie Drubetskáya as she collected and pressed together a bunch of raveled lint with her thin, beringed fingers.

Julie was preparing to leave Moscow next day and was giving a farewell soiree.

"*Bezúkhovest ridicule*, but he is so kind and good-natured. What pleasure is there to be so *caustique?*"

"A forfeit!" cried a young man in militia uniform whom Julie called *"mon chevalier,"* and who was going with her to Nízhni.

In Julie's set, as in many other circles in Moscow, it had been agreed that they would speak nothing but Russian and that those who made a slip and spoke French should pay fines to the Committee of Voluntary Contributions.

"Another forfeit for a Gallicism," said a Russian writer who was present. "'What pleasure is there to be' is not Russian!"

"You spare no one," continued Julie to the young man without heeding the author's remark.

"For *caustique*—I am guilty and will pay, and I am prepared to pay again for the pleasure of telling you the truth. For Gallicisms I won't be responsible," she remarked, turning to the author: "I have neither the money nor the time, like Prince Galítsyn, to engage a master to teach me Russian!"

"Ah, here he is!" she added. "*Quand on...* No, no," she said to the militia officer, "you won't catch me. Speak of the sun and you see its rays!" and she smiled amiably at Pierre. "We were just talking of you," she said with the facility in lying natural to a society woman. "We were saying that your regiment would be sure to be better than Mamónov's."

"Oh, don't talk to me of my regiment," replied Pierre, kissing his hostess' hand and taking a seat beside her. "I am so sick of it."

"You will, of course, command it yourself?" said Julie, directing a sly, sarcastic glance toward the militia officer.

The latter in Pierre's presence had ceased to be caustic, and his face expressed perplexity as to what Julie's smile might mean. In spite of his absent-mindedness and good nature, Pierre's personality immediately checked any attempt to ridicule him to his face.

"No," said Pierre, with a laughing glance at his big, stout body. "I should make too good a target for the French, besides I am afraid I should hardly be able to climb onto a horse."

Among those whom Julie's guests happened to choose to gossip about were the Rostóvs.

"I hear that their affairs are in a very bad way," said Julie. "And he is so unreasonable, the count himself I mean. The Razumóvskis wanted to buy his house and his estate near Moscow, but it drags on and on. He asks too much."

"No, I think the sale will come off in a few days," said someone. "Though it is madness to buy anything in Moscow now."

"Why?" asked Julie. "You don't think Moscow is in danger?"

"Then why are you leaving?"

"I? What a question! I am going because... well, because everyone is going: and besides—I am not Joan of Arc or an Amazon."

"Well, of course, of course! Let me have some more strips of linen."

"If he manages the business properly he will be able to pay off all his debts," said the militia officer, speaking of Rostóv.

"A kindly old man but not up to much. And why do they stay on so long in Moscow? They meant to leave for the country long ago. Natalie is quite well again now, isn't she?" Julie asked Pierre with a knowing smile.

"They are waiting for their younger son," Pierre replied. "He joined Obolénski's Cossacks and went to BélayaTsérkov where the regiment is being formed. But now they have had him transferred to my regiment and are expecting him every day. The count wanted to leave long ago, but the countess won't on any account leave Moscow till her son returns."

"I met them the day before yesterday at the Arkhárovs'. Natalie has recovered her looks and is brighter. She sang a song. How easily some people get over everything!"

"Get over what?" inquired Pierre, looking displeased.

Julie smiled.

"You know, Count, such knights as you are only found in Madame de Souza's novels."

"What knights? What do you mean?" demanded Pierre, blushing.

"Oh, come, my dear count! *C'est la fable de tout Moscou. Je vous admire, ma parole d'honneur!*" *

* "It is the talk of all Moscow. My word, I admire you!"

"Forfeit, forfeit!" cried the militia officer.

"All right, one can't talk—how tiresome!"

"What is 'the talk of all Moscow'?" Pierre asked angrily, rising to his feet.

"Come now, Count, you know!"

"I don't know anything about it," said Pierre.

"I know you were friendly with Natalie, and so... but I was always more friendly with Véra—that dear Véra."

"No, madame!" Pierre continued in a tone of displeasure, "I have not taken on myself the role of Natalie Rostóva's knight at all, and have not been to their house for nearly a month. But I cannot understand the cruelty..."

"*Qui s'excuses'accuse,*" * said Julie, smiling and waving the lint triumphantly, and to have the last word she promptly changed the subject. "Do you know what I heard today? Poor Mary Bolkónskaya arrived in Moscow yesterday. Do you know that she has lost her father?"

* "Who excuses himself, accuses himself."

"Really? Where is she? I should like very much to see her," said Pierre.

"I spent the evening with her yesterday. She is going to their estate near Moscow either today or tomorrow morning, with her nephew."

"Well, and how is she?" asked Pierre.

"She is well, but sad. But do you know who rescued her? It is quite a romance. Nicholas Rostóv! She was surrounded, and they wanted to kill her and had wounded some of her people. He rushed in and saved her...."

"Another romance," said the militia officer. "Really, this general flight has been arranged to get all the old maids married off. Catiche is one and Princess Bolkónskaya another."

"Do you know, I really believe she is *un petit peuamoureuse du jeune homme.*" *

* "A little bit in love with the young man."

"Forfeit, forfeit, forfeit!"

"But how could one say that in Russian?"

CHAPTER XVIII

W hen Pierre returned home he was handed two of Rostopchín's broadsheets that had been brought that day.

The first declared that the report that Count Rostopchín had forbidden people to leave Moscow was false; on the contrary he was glad that ladies and tradesmen's wives were leaving the city. "There will be less panic and less gossip," ran the broadsheet "but I will stake my life on it that that scoundrel will not enter Moscow." These words showed Pierre clearly for the first time that the French would enter Moscow. The second broadsheet stated that our headquarters were at Vyázma, that Count Wittgenstein had defeated the French, but that as many of the inhabitants of Moscow wished to be armed, weapons were ready for them at the arsenal: sabers, pistols, and muskets which could be had at a low price. The tone of the proclamation was not as jocose as in the former Chigírin talks. Pierre pondered over these broadsheets. Evidently the terrible stormcloud he had desired with the whole strength of his soul but which yet aroused involuntary horror in him was drawing near.

"Shall I join the army and enter the service, or wait?" he asked himself for the hundredth time. He took a pack of cards that lay on the table and began to lay them out for a game of patience.

"If this patience comes out," he said to himself after shuffling the cards, holding them in his hand, and lifting his head, "if it comes out, it means... what does it mean?"

He had not decided what it should mean when he heard the voice of the eldest princess at the door asking whether she might come in.

"Then it will mean that I must go to the army," said Pierre to himself. "Come in, come in!" he added to the princess.

Only the eldest princess, the one with the stony face and long waist, was still living in Pierre's house. The two younger ones had both married.

"Excuse my coming to you, cousin," she said in a reproachful and agitated voice. "You know some decision must be come to. What is going to happen? Everyone has left Moscow and the people are rioting. How is it that we are staying on?"

"On the contrary, things seem satisfactory, *ma cousine*," said Pierre in the bantering tone he habitually adopted toward her, always feeling uncomfortable in the role of her benefactor.

"Satisfactory, indeed! Very satisfactory! Barbara Ivánovna told me today how our troops are distinguishing themselves. It certainly does them credit! And the people too are quite mutinous—they no longer obey, even my maid has taken to being rude. At this rate they will soon begin beating us. One can't walk in the streets. But, above all, the French will be here any day now, so what are we waiting for? I ask just one thing of you, cousin," she went on, "arrange for me to be taken to Petersburg. Whatever I may be, I can't live under Bonaparte's rule."

"Oh, come, *ma cousine!* Where do you get your information from? On the contrary..."

"I won't submit to your Napoleon! Others may if they please.... If you don't want to do this..."

"But I will, I'll give the order at once."

The princess was apparently vexed at not having anyone to be angry with. Muttering to herself, she sat down on a chair.

"But you have been misinformed," said Pierre. "Everything is quiet in the city and there is not the slightest danger. See! I've just been reading..." He showed her the broadsheet. "Count Rostopchín writes that he will stake his life on it that the enemy will not enter Moscow."

"Oh, that count of yours!" said the princess malevolently. "He is a hypocrite, a rascal who has himself roused the people to riot. Didn't he write in those idiotic broadsheets that anyone, 'whoever it might be, should be dragged to the lockup by his hair'? (How silly!) 'And honor and glory to whoever captures him,' he says. This is what his cajolery has brought us to! Barbara Ivánovna told me the mob near killed her because she said something in French."

"Oh, but it's so... You take everything so to heart," said Pierre, and began laying out his cards for patience.

Although that patience did come out, Pierre did not join the army, but remained in deserted Moscow ever in the same state of agitation, irresolution, and alarm, yet at the same time joyfully expecting something terrible.

Next day toward evening the princess set off, and Pierre's head steward came to inform him that the money needed for the equipment of his regiment could not be found without selling one of the estates. In general the head steward made out to Pierre that his project of raising a regiment would ruin him. Pierre listened to him, scarcely able to repress a smile.

"Well then, sell it," said he. "What's to be done? I can't draw back now!"

The worse everything became, especially his own affairs, the better was Pierre pleased and the more evident was it that the catastrophe he expected was approaching. Hardly anyone he knew was left in town. Julie had gone, and so had Princess Mary. Of his intimate friends only the Rostóvs remained, but he did not go to see them.

To distract his thoughts he drove that day to the village of Vorontsóvo to see the great balloon Leppich was constructing to destroy the foe, and a trial balloon that was to go up next day. The balloon was not yet ready, but Pierre learned that it was being constructed by the Emperor's desire. The Emperor had written to Count Rostopchín as follows:

As soon as Leppich is ready, get together a crew of reliable and intelligent men for his car and send a courier to General Kutúzov to let him know. I have informed him of the matter.

Please impress upon Leppich to be very careful where he descends for the first time, that he may not make a mistake and fall into the enemy's hands. It is essential for him to combine his movements with those of the commander in chief.

On his way home from Vorontsóvo, as he was passing the Bolótnoe Place Pierre, seeing a large crowd round the Lóbnoe Place, stopped and got out of his trap. A French cook accused of being a spy was being flogged. The flogging was only just over, and the executioner was releasing from the flogging bench a stout man with red whiskers, in blue stockings and a green jacket, who was moaning piteously. Another criminal, thin and pale, stood near. Judging by their faces they were both Frenchmen. With a frightened and suffering look resembling that on the thin Frenchman's face, Pierre pushed his way in through the crowd.

"What is it? Who is it? What is it for?" he kept asking.

But the attention of the crowd—officials, burghers, shopkeepers, peasants, and women in cloaks and in pelisses—was so eagerly centered on what was passing in Lóbnoe Place that no one answered him. The stout man rose, frowned, shrugged his shoulders, and evidently trying to appear firm began to pull on his jacket without looking about him, but suddenly his lips trembled and he began to cry, in the way full-blooded grown-up men cry, though angry with himself for doing so. In the crowd people began talking loudly, to stifle their feelings of pity as it seemed to Pierre.

"He's cook to some prince."

"Eh, mounseer, Russian sauce seems to be sour to a Frenchman... sets his teeth on edge!" said a wrinkled clerk who was standing behind Pierre, when the Frenchman began to cry.

The clerk glanced round, evidently hoping that his joke would be appreciated. Some people began to laugh, others continued to watch in dismay the executioner who was undressing the other man.

Pierre choked, his face puckered, and he turned hastily away, went back to his trap muttering something to himself as he went, and took his seat. As they drove along he shuddered and exclaimed several times so audibly that the coachman asked him:

"What is your pleasure?"

"Where are you going?" shouted Pierre to the man, who was driving to Lubyánka Street.

"To the Governor's, as you ordered," answered the coachman.

"Fool! Idiot!" shouted Pierre, abusing his coachman—a thing he rarely did. "Home, I told you! And drive faster, blockhead!" "I must get away this very day," he murmured to himself.

At the sight of the tortured Frenchman and the crowd surrounding the Lóbnoe Place, Pierre had so definitely made up his mind that he could no longer remain in Moscow and would leave for the army that very day that it seemed to him that either he had told the coachman this or that the man ought to have known it for himself.

On reaching home Pierre gave orders to Evstáfey—his head coachman who knew everything, could do anything, and was known to all Moscow—that he would leave that night for the army at Mozháysk, and that his saddle horses should be sent there. This could not all be arranged that day, so on Evstáfey's representation Pierre had to put off his departure till next day to allow time for the relay horses to be sent on in advance.

On the twenty-fourth the weather cleared up after a spell of rain, and after dinner Pierre left Moscow. When changing horses that night in Perkhúshkovo, he learned that there had been a great battle that evening. (This was the battle of Shevárdino.) He was told that there in Perkhúshkovo the earth trembled from the firing, but nobody could answer his questions as to who had won. At dawn next day Pierre was approaching Mozháysk.

Every house in Mozháysk had soldiers quartered in it, and at the hostel where Pierre was met by his groom and coachman there was no room to be had. It was full of officers.

Everywhere in Mozháysk and beyond it, troops were stationed or on the march. Cossacks, foot and horse soldiers, wagons, caissons, and cannon were everywhere. Pierre pushed forward as fast as he could, and the farther he left Moscow behind and the deeper he plunged into that sea of troops the more was he overcome by restless agitation and a new and joyful feeling he had not experienced before. It was a feeling akin to what he had felt at the Slobóda Palace during the Emperor's visit—a sense of the necessity of undertaking something and sacrificing something. He now experienced a glad consciousness that everything that constitutes men's happiness— the comforts of life, wealth, even life itself—is rubbish it is pleasant to throw away, compared with something... With what? Pierre could not say, and he did not try to determine for whom and for what he felt such particular delight in sacrificing everything. He was not occupied with the question of what to sacrifice for; the fact of sacrificing in itself afforded him a new and joyous sensation.

CHAPTER XIX

On the twenty-fourth of August the battle of the Shevárdino Redoubt was fought, on the twenty-fifth not a shot was fired by either side, and on the twenty-sixth the battle of Borodinó itself took place.

Why and how were the battles of Shevárdino and Borodinó given and accepted? Why was the battle of Borodinó fought? There was not the least sense in it for either the French or the Russians. Its immediate result for the Russians was, and was bound to be, that we were brought nearer to the destruction of Moscow—which we feared more than anything in the world; and for the French its immediate result was that they were brought nearer to the destruction of their whole army—which they feared more than anything in the world. What the result must be was quite obvious, and yet Napoleon offered and Kutúzov accepted that battle.

If the commanders had been guided by reason, it would seem that it must have been obvious to Napoleon that by advancing thirteen hundred miles and giving battle with a probability of losing a quarter of his army, he was advancing to certain destruction, and it must have been equally clear to Kutúzov that by accepting battle and risking the loss of a quarter of his army he would certainly lose Moscow. For Kutúzov this was mathematically clear, as it is that if when playing draughts I have one man less and go on exchanging, I shall certainly lose, and therefore should not exchange. When my opponent has sixteen men and I have fourteen, I am only one eighth weaker than he, but when I have exchanged thirteen more men he will be three times as strong as I am.

Before the battle of Borodinó our strength in proportion to the French was about as five to six, but after that battle it was little more than one to two: previously we had a hundred thousand against a hundred and twenty thousand; afterwards little more than fifty thousand against a hundred thousand. Yet the shrewd and experienced Kutúzov accepted the battle, while Napoleon, who was said to be a commander of genius, gave it, losing a quarter of his army and lengthening his lines of communication still more. If it is said that he expected to end the campaign by occupying Moscow as he had ended a previous campaign by occupying Vienna, there is much evidence to the contrary. Napoleon's historians themselves tell us that from Smolénsk onwards he wished to stop, knew the danger of his extended position, and knew that the occupation of Moscow would not be the end of the campaign, for he had seen at Smolénsk the state in which Russian towns were left to him, and had not received a single reply to his repeated announcements of his wish to negotiate.

In giving and accepting battle at Borodinó, Kutúzov acted involuntarily and irrationally. But later on, to fit what had occurred, the historians provided cunningly devised evidence of the foresight and genius of the generals who, of all the blind tools of history were the most enslaved and involuntary.

The ancients have left us model heroic poems in which the heroes furnish the whole interest of the story, and we are still unable to accustom ourselves to the fact that for our epoch histories of that kind are meaningless.

On the other question, how the battle of Borodinó and the preceding battle of Shevárdino were fought, there also exists a definite and well-known, but quite false, conception. All the historians describe the affair as follows:

The Russian army, they say, in its retreat from Smolénsk sought out for itself the best position for a general engagement and found such a position at Borodinó.

The Russians, they say, fortified this position in advance on the left of the highroad (from Moscow to Smolénsk) and almost at a right angle to it, from Borodinó to Utítsa, at the very place where the battle was fought.

In front of this position, they say, a fortified outpost was set up on the Shevárdino mound to observe the enemy. On the twenty-fourth, we are told, *Napoleon attacked this advanced post and took it, and, on the twenty-sixth, attacked the whole Russian army, which was in position on the field of Borodinó.*

So the histories say, and it is all quite wrong, as anyone who cares to look into the matter can easily convince himself.

The Russians did not seek out the best position but, on the contrary, during the retreat passed many positions better than Borodinó. They did not stop at any one of these positions because Kutúzov did not wish to occupy a position he had not himself chosen, because the popular demand for a battle had not yet expressed itself strongly enough, and because Milorádovich had not yet arrived with the militia, and for many other reasons. The fact is that other positions they had passed were stronger, and that the position at Borodinó (the one where the battle was fought), far from being strong, was no more a *position* than any other spot one might find in the Russian Empire by sticking a pin into the map at hazard.

Not only did the Russians not fortify the position on the field of Borodinó to the left of, and at a right angle to, the highroad (that is, the position on which the battle took place), but never till the twenty-fifth of August, 1812, did they think that a battle might be fought there. This was shown first by the fact that there were no entrenchments there by the twenty fifth and that those begun on the twenty-fifth and twenty-sixth were not completed, and secondly, by the position of the Shevárdino Redoubt. That redoubt was quite senseless in front of the position where the battle was accepted. Why was it more strongly fortified than any other post? And why were all efforts exhausted and six thousand men sacrificed to defend it till late at night on the twenty-fourth? A Cossack patrol would have sufficed to observe the enemy. Thirdly, as proof that the position on which the battle was fought had not been foreseen and that the Shevárdino Redoubt was not an advanced post of that position, we have the fact that up to the twenty-fifth, Barclay de Tolly and Bagratión were convinced that the Shevárdino Redoubt was the *left flank* of the position, and that Kutúzov himself in his report, written in hot haste after the battle, speaks of the Shevárdino Redoubt as the *left flank* of the position. It was much later, when reports on the battle of Borodinó were written at leisure, that the incorrect and extraordinary statement was invented (probably to justify the mistakes of a commander in chief who had to be represented as infallible) that the Shevárdino Redoubt was an *advanced* post—whereas in reality it was simply a fortified point on the left flank—and that the battle of Borodinó was fought by us on an entrenched position previously selected, whereas it was fought on a quite unexpected spot which was almost unentrenched.

The case was evidently this: a position was selected along the river Kolochá—which crosses the highroad not at a right angle but at an acute angle—so that the left flank was at Shevárdino, the right flank near the village of Nóvoe, and the center at Borodinó at the confluence of the rivers Kolochá and Vóyna.

To anyone who looks at the field of Borodinó without thinking of how the battle was actually fought, this position, protected by the river Kolochá, presents itself as obvious for an army whose object was to prevent an enemy from advancing along the Smolénsk road to Moscow.

Napoleon, riding to Valúevo on the twenty-fourth, did not see (as the history books say he did) the position of the Russians from Utítsa to Borodinó (he could not have seen that position because it did not exist), nor did he see an advanced post of the Russian army, but while pursuing the Russian rearguard he came upon the left flank of the Russian position—at the Shevárdino Redoubt—and unexpectedly for the Russians moved his army across the Kolochá. And the Russians, not having time to begin a general engagement, withdrew their left wing from the position they had intended to occupy and took up a new position which had not been foreseen and was not fortified. By crossing to the other side of the Kolochá to the left of the highroad, Napoleon shifted the whole forthcoming battle from right to left (looking from the Russian side) and transferred it to the plain between Utítsa, Semënovsk, and Borodinó—a plain no more advantageous as a position than any other plain in Russia—and there the whole battle of the twenty-sixth of August took place.

Had Napoleon not ridden out on the evening of the twenty-fourth to the Kolochá, and had he not then ordered an immediate attack on the redoubt but had begun the attack next morning, no one would have doubted that the ShevárdinoRedoubt was the left flank of our position, and the battle would have taken place where we expected it. In that case we should probably have defended the Shevárdino Redoubt—our left flank—still more obstinately. We should have attacked Napoleon in the center or on the right, and the engagement would have taken place on the twenty-fifth, in the position we intended and had fortified. But as the attack on our left flank took place in the evening after the retreat of our rear guard (that is, immediately after the fight at Gridnëva), and as the Russian commanders did not wish, or were not in time, to begin a general engagement then on the evening of the twenty-fourth, the first and chief action of the battle of Borodinó was already lost on the twenty-fourth, and obviously led to the loss of the one fought on the twenty-sixth.

After the loss of the Shevárdino Redoubt, we found ourselves on the morning of the twenty-fifth without a position for our left flank, and were forced to bend it back and hastily entrench it where it chanced to be.

Not only was the Russian army on the twenty-sixth defended by weak, unfinished entrenchments, but the disadvantage of that position was increased by the fact that the Russian commanders—not having fully realized what had happened, namely the loss of our position on the left flank and the shifting of the whole field of the forthcoming battle from right to left—maintained their extended position from the village of Nóvoe to Utítsa, and consequently had to move their forces from right to left during the battle. So it happened that throughout the whole battle the Russians opposed the entire French army launched against our left flank with but half as many men. (Poniatowski's action against Utítsa, and Uvárov's on the right flank against the French, were actions distinct from the main course of the battle.) So the battle of Borodinó did not take place at all as (in an effort to conceal our commanders' mistakes even at the cost of diminishing the glory due to the Russian army and people) it has been described. The battle of Borodinó was not fought on a chosen and entrenched position with forces only slightly weaker than those of the enemy, but, as a result of the loss of the Shevárdino Redoubt, the Russians fought the battle of Borodinó on an open and almost unentrenched position, with forces only half as numerous as the French; that is to say, under conditions in which it was not merely unthinkable to fight for ten hours and secure an indecisive result, but unthinkable to keep an army even from complete disintegration and flight.

War and Peace

CHAPTER XX

O n the morning of the twenty-fifth Pierre was leaving Mozháysk. At the descent of the high steep hill, down which a winding road led out of the town past the cathedral on the right, where a service was being held and the bells were ringing, Pierre got out of his vehicle and proceeded on foot. Behind him a cavalry regiment was coming down the hill preceded by its singers. Coming up toward him was a train of carts carrying men who had been wounded in the engagement the day before. The peasant drivers, shouting and lashing their horses, kept crossing from side to side. The carts, in each of which three or four wounded soldiers were lying or sitting, jolted over the stones that had been thrown on the steep incline to make it something like a road. The wounded, bandaged with rags, with pale cheeks, compressed lips, and knitted brows, held on to the sides of the carts as they were jolted against one another. Almost all of them stared with naïve, childlike curiosity at Pierre's white hat and green swallow-tail coat.

Pierre's coachman shouted angrily at the convoy of wounded to keep to one side of the road. The cavalry regiment, as it descended the hill with its singers, surrounded Pierre's carriage and blocked the road. Pierre stopped, being pressed against the side of the cutting in which the road ran. The sunshine from behind the hill did not penetrate into the cutting and there it was cold and damp, but above Pierre's head was the bright August sunshine and the bells sounded merrily. One of the carts with wounded stopped by the side of the road close to Pierre. The driver in his bast shoes ran panting up to it, placed a stone under one of its tireless hind wheels, and began arranging the breech-band on his little horse.

One of the wounded, an old soldier with a bandaged arm who was following the cart on foot, caught hold of it with his sound hand and turned to look at Pierre.

"I say, fellow countryman! Will they set us down here or take us on to Moscow?" he asked.

Pierre was so deep in thought that he did not hear the question. He was looking now at the cavalry regiment that had met the convoy of wounded, now at the cart by which he was standing, in which two wounded men were sitting and one was lying. One of those sitting up in the cart had probably been wounded in the cheek. His whole head was wrapped in rags and one cheek was swollen to the size of a baby's head. His nose and mouth were twisted to one side. This soldier was looking at the cathedral and crossing himself. Another, a young lad, a fair-haired recruit as white as though there was no blood in his thin face, looked at Pierre kindly, with a fixed smile. The third lay prone so that his face was not visible. The cavalry singers were passing close by:

Ah lost, quite lost... is my head so keen, Living in a foreign land...

they sang their soldiers' dance song.

As if responding to them but with a different sort of merriment, the metallic sound of the bells reverberated high above and the hot rays of the sun bathed the top of the opposite slope with yet another sort of merriment. But beneath the slope, by the cart with the wounded near the panting little nag where Pierre stood, it was damp, somber, and sad.

The soldier with the swollen cheek looked angrily at the cavalry singers.

"Oh, the coxcombs!" he muttered reproachfully.

"It's not the soldiers only, but I've seen peasants today, too.... The peasants—even they have to go," said the soldier behind the cart, addressing Pierre with a sad smile. "No distinctions made nowadays.... They want the whole nation to fall on them—in a word, it's Moscow! They want to make an end of it."

In spite of the obscurity of the soldier's words Pierre understood what he wanted to say and nodded approval.

The road was clear again; Pierre descended the hill and drove on.

He kept looking to either side of the road for familiar faces, but only saw everywhere the unfamiliar faces of various military men of different branches of the service, who all looked with astonishment at his white hat and green tail coat.

Having gone nearly three miles he at last met an acquaintance and eagerly addressed him. This was one of the head army doctors. He was driving toward Pierre in a covered gig, sitting beside a young surgeon, and on recognizing Pierre he told the Cossack who occupied the driver's seat to pull up.

"Count! Your excellency, how come you to be here?" asked the doctor.

"Well, you know, I wanted to see..."

"Yes, yes, there will be something to see...."

Pierre got out and talked to the doctor, explaining his intention of taking part in a battle.

The doctor advised him to apply direct to Kutúzov.

"Why should you be God knows where out of sight, during the battle?" he said, exchanging glances with his young companion. "Anyhow his Serene Highness knows you and will receive you graciously. That's what you must do."

The doctor seemed tired and in a hurry.

"You think so?... Ah, I also wanted to ask you where our position is exactly?" said Pierre.

"The position?" repeated the doctor. "Well, that's not my line. Drive past Tatárinova, a lot of digging is going on there. Go up the hillock and you'll see."

"Can one see from there?... If you would..."

But the doctor interrupted him and moved toward his gig.

"I would go with you but on my honor I'm up to here"—and he pointed to his throat. "I'm galloping to the commander of the corps. How do matters stand?... You know, Count, there'll be a battle tomorrow. Out of an army of a hundred thousand we must expect at least twenty thousand wounded, and we haven't stretchers, or bunks, or dressers, or doctors enough for six thousand. We have ten thousand carts, but we need other things as well—we must manage as best we can!"

The strange thought that of the thousands of men, young and old, who had stared with merry surprise at his hat (perhaps the very men he had noticed), twenty thousand were inevitably doomed to wounds and death amazed Pierre.

"They may die tomorrow; why are they thinking of anything but death?" And by some latent sequence of thought the descent of the Mozháysk hill, the carts with the wounded, the ringing bells, the slanting rays of the sun, and the songs of the cavalrymen vividly recurred to his mind.

"The cavalry ride to battle and meet the wounded and do not for a moment think of what awaits them, but pass by, winking at the wounded. Yet from among these men twenty thousand are doomed to die, and they wonder at my hat! Strange!" thought Pierre, continuing his way to Tatárinova.

In front of a landowner's house to the left of the road stood carriages, wagons, and crowds of orderlies and sentinels. The commander in chief was putting up there, but just when Pierre arrived he was not in and hardly any of the staff were there—they had gone to the church service. Pierre drove on toward Górki.

When he had ascended the hill and reached the little village street, he saw for the first time peasant militiamen in their white shirts and with crosses on their caps, who, talking and laughing loudly, animated and perspiring, were at work on a huge knoll overgrown with grass to the right of the road.

Some of them were digging, others were wheeling barrowloads of earth along planks, while others stood about doing nothing.

Two officers were standing on the knoll, directing the men. On seeing these peasants, who were evidently still amused by the novelty of their position as soldiers, Pierre once more thought of the wounded men at Mozháysk and understood what the soldier had meant when he said: "They want the whole nation to fall on them." The sight of these bearded peasants at work on the battlefield, with their queer, clumsy boots and perspiring necks, and their shirts opening from the left toward the middle, unfastened, exposing their sunburned collarbones, impressed Pierre more strongly with the solemnity and importance of the moment than anything he had yet seen or heard.

CHAPTER XXI

Pierre stepped out of his carriage and, passing the toiling militiamen, ascended the knoll from which, according to the doctor, the battlefield could be seen.

It was about eleven o'clock. The sun shone somewhat to the left and behind him and brightly lit up the enormous panorama which, rising like an amphitheater, extended before him in the clear rarefied atmosphere.

From above on the left, bisecting that amphitheater, wound the Smolénsk highroad, passing through a village with a white church some five hundred paces in front of the knoll and below it. This was Borodinó. Below the village the road crossed the river by a bridge and, winding down and up, rose higher and higher to the village of Valúevo visible about four miles away, where Napoleon was then stationed. Beyond Valúevo the road disappeared into a yellowing forest on the horizon. Far in the distance in that birch and fir forest to the right of the road, the cross and belfry of the Kolochá Monastery gleamed in the sun. Here and there over the whole of that blue expanse, to right and left of the forest and the road, smoking campfires could be seen and indefinite masses of troops—ours and the enemy's. The ground to the right—along the course of the Kolochá and Moskvá rivers—was broken and hilly. Between the hollows the villages of Bezúbova and Zakhárino showed in the distance. On the left the ground was more level; there were fields of grain, and the smoking ruins of Semënovsk, which had been burned down, could be seen.

All that Pierre saw was so indefinite that neither the left nor the right side of the field fully satisfied his expectations. Nowhere could he see the battlefield he had expected to find, but only fields, meadows, troops, woods, the smoke of campfires, villages, mounds, and streams; and try as he would he could descry no military "position" in this place which teemed with life, nor could he even distinguish our troops from the enemy's.

"I must ask someone who knows," he thought, and addressed an officer who was looking with curiosity at his huge unmilitary figure.

"May I ask you," said Pierre, "what village that is in front?"

"Búrdino, isn't it?" said the officer, turning to his companion.

"Borodinó," the other corrected him.

The officer, evidently glad of an opportunity for a talk, moved up to Pierre.

"Are those our men there?" Pierre inquired.

"Yes, and there, further on, are the French," said the officer. "There they are, there... you can see them."

"Where? Where?" asked Pierre.

"One can see them with the naked eye... Why, there!"

The officer pointed with his hand to the smoke visible on the left beyond the river, and the same stern and serious expression that Pierre had noticed on many of the faces he had met came into his face.

"Ah, those are the French! And over there?..." Pierre pointed to a knoll on the left, near which some troops could be seen.

"Those are ours."

"Ah, ours! And there?..." Pierre pointed to another knoll in the distance with a big tree on it, near a village that lay in a hollow where also some campfires were smoking and something black was visible.

"That's *his* again," said the officer. (It was the Shevárdino Redoubt.) "It was ours yesterday, but now it is *his*."

"Then how about our position?"

"Our position?" replied the officer with a smile of satisfaction. "I can tell you quite clearly, because I constructed nearly all our entrenchments. There, you see? There's our center, at Borodinó, just there," and he pointed to the village in front of them with the white church. "That's where one crosses the Kolochá. You see down there where the rows of hay are lying in the hollow, there's the bridge. That's our center. Our right flank is over there"—he pointed sharply to the right, far away in the broken ground—"That's where the Moskvá River is, and we have thrown up three redoubts there, very strong ones. The left flank..." here the officer paused. "Well, you see, that's difficult to explain.... Yesterday our left flank was there at Shevárdino, you see, where the oak is, but now we have withdrawn our left wing—now it is over there, do you see that village and the smoke? That's Semënovsk, yes, there," he pointed to Raévski's knoll. "But the battle will hardly be there. *His* having moved his troops there is only a ruse; *he* will probably pass round to the right of the Moskvá. But wherever it may be, many a man will be missing tomorrow!" he remarked.

An elderly sergeant who had approached the officer while he was giving these explanations had waited in silence for him to finish speaking, but at this point, evidently not liking the officer's remark, interrupted him.

"Gabions must be sent for," said he sternly.

The officer appeared abashed, as though he understood that one might think of how many men would be missing tomorrow but ought not to speak of it.

"Well, send number three company again," the officer replied hurriedly.

"And you, are you one of the doctors?"

"No, I've come on my own," answered Pierre, and he went down the hill again, passing the militiamen.

"Oh, those damned fellows!" muttered the officer who followed him, holding his nose as he ran past the men at work.

"There they are... bringing her, coming... There they are... They'll be here in a minute..." voices were suddenly heard saying; and officers, soldiers, and militiamen began running forward along the road.

A church procession was coming up the hill from Borodinó. First along the dusty road came the infantry in ranks, bareheaded and with arms reversed. From behind them came the sound of church singing.

Soldiers and militiamen ran bareheaded past Pierre toward the procession.

"They are bringing her, our Protectress!... The Iberian Mother of God!" someone cried.

"The Smolénsk Mother of God," another corrected him.

The militiamen, both those who had been in the village and those who had been at work on the battery, threw down their spades and ran to meet the church procession. Following the battalion that marched along the dusty road came priests in their vestments—one little old man in a hood with attendants and singers. Behind them soldiers and officers bore a large, dark-faced icon with an embossed metal cover. This was the icon that had been brought from Smolénsk and had since accompanied the army. Behind, before, and on both sides, crowds of militiamen with bared heads walked, ran, and bowed to the ground.

At the summit of the hill they stopped with the icon; the men who had been holding it up by the linen bands attached to it were relieved by others, the chanters relit their censers, and service began. The hot rays of the sun beat down vertically and a fresh soft wind played with the hair of the bared heads and with the ribbons decorating the icon. The singing did not sound loud under the open sky. An immense crowd of bareheaded officers, soldiers, and militiamen surrounded the icon. Behind the priest and a chanter stood the notabilities on a spot reserved for them. A bald general with a St. George's Cross on his neck stood just behind the priest's back, and without crossing himself (he was evidently a German) patiently awaited the end of the service, which he considered it necessary to hear to the end, probably to arouse the patriotism of the Russian people. Another general stood in a martial pose, crossing himself by shaking his hand in front of his chest while looking about him. Standing among the crowd of peasants, Pierre recognized several acquaintances among these notables, but did not look at them—his whole attention was absorbed in watching the serious expression on the faces of the crowd of soldiers and militiamen who were all gazing eagerly at the icon. As soon as the tired chanters, who were singing the service for the twentieth time that day, began lazily and mechanically to sing: "Save from calamity Thy servants, O Mother of God," and the priest and deacon chimed in: "For to Thee under God we all flee as to an inviolable bulwark and protection," there again kindled in all those faces the same expression of consciousness of the solemnity of the impending moment that Pierre had seen on the faces at the foot of the hill at Mozháysk and momentarily on many and many faces he had met that morning; and heads were bowed more frequently and hair tossed back, and sighs and the sound men made as they crossed themselves were heard.

The crowd round the icon suddenly parted and pressed against Pierre. Someone, a very important personage judging by the haste with which way was made for him, was approaching the icon.

It was Kutúzov, who had been riding round the position and on his way back to Tatárinova had stopped where the service was being held. Pierre recognized him at once by his peculiar figure, which distinguished him from everybody else.

With a long overcoat on his exceedingly stout, round-shouldered body, with uncovered white head and puffy face showing the white ball of the eye he had lost, Kutúzov walked with plunging, swaying gait into the crowd and stopped behind the priest. He crossed himself with an accustomed movement, bent till he touched the ground with his hand, and bowed his white head with a deep sigh. Behind Kutúzov was Bennigsen and the suite. Despite the presence of the commander in chief, who attracted the attention of all the superior officers, the militiamen and soldiers continued their prayers without looking at him.

When the service was over, Kutúzov stepped up to the icon, sank heavily to his knees, bowed to the ground, and for a long time tried vainly to rise, but could not do so on account of his weakness and weight. His white head twitched with the effort. At last he rose, kissed the icon as a child does with naïvely pouting lips, and again bowed till he touched the ground with his hand. The other generals followed his example, then the officers, and after them with excited faces, pressing on one another, crowding, panting, and pushing, scrambled the soldiers and militiamen.

CHAPTER XXII

S taggering amid the crush, Pierre looked about him.

"Count Peter Kirílovich! How did you get here?" said a voice.

Pierre looked round. BorísDrubetskóy, brushing his knees with his hand (he had probably soiled them when he, too, had knelt before the icon), came up to him smiling. Borís was elegantly dressed, with a slightly martial touch appropriate to a campaign. He wore a long coat and like Kutúzov had a whip slung across his shoulder.

Meanwhile Kutúzov had reached the village and seated himself in the shade of the nearest house, on a bench which one Cossack had run to fetch and another had hastily covered with a rug. An immense and brilliant suite surrounded him.

The icon was carried further, accompanied by the throng. Pierre stopped some thirty paces from Kutúzov, talking to Borís.

He explained his wish to be present at the battle and to see the position.

"This is what you must do," said Borís. "I will do the honors of the camp to you. You will see everything best from where Count Bennigsen will be. I am in attendance on him, you know; I'll mention it to him. But if you want to ride round the position, come along with us. We are just going to the left flank. Then when we get back, do spend the night with me and we'll arrange a game of cards. Of course you know DmítriSergéevich? Those are his quarters," and he pointed to the third house in the village of Górki.

"But I should like to see the right flank. They say it's very strong," said Pierre. "I should like to start from the Moskvá River and ride round the whole position."

"Well, you can do that later, but the chief thing is the left flank."

"Yes, yes. But where is Prince Bolkónski's regiment? Can you point it out to me?"

"Prince Andrew's? We shall pass it and I'll take you to him."

"What about the left flank?" asked Pierre

"To tell you the truth, between ourselves, God only knows what state our left flank is in," said Borís confidentially lowering his voice. "It is not at all what Count Bennigsen intended. He meant to fortify that knoll quite differently, but..." Borís shrugged his shoulders, "his Serene Highness would not have it, or someone persuaded him. You see..." but Borís did not finish, for at that moment Kaysárov, Kutúzov's adjutant, came up to Pierre. "Ah, Kaysárov!" said Borís, addressing him with an unembarrassed smile, "I was just trying to explain our position to the count. It is amazing how his Serene Highness could so foresee the intentions of the French!"

"You mean the left flank?" asked Kaysárov.

"Yes, exactly; the left flank is now extremely strong."

Though Kutúzov had dismissed all unnecessary men from the staff, Borís had contrived to remain at headquarters after the changes. He had established himself with Count Bennigsen, who, like all on whom Borís had been in attendance, considered young Prince Drubetskóy an invaluable man.

In the higher command there were two sharply defined parties: Kutúzov's party and that of Bennigsen, the chief of staff. Borís belonged to the latter and no one else, while showing servile respect to Kutúzov, could so create an impression that the old fellow was not much good and that Bennigsen managed everything. Now the decisive moment of battle had come when Kutúzov would be destroyed and the power pass to Bennigsen, or even if Kutúzov won the battle it would be felt that everything was done by Bennigsen. In any case many great rewards would have to be given for tomorrow's action, and new men would come to the front. So Borís was full of nervous vivacity all day.

After Kaysárov, others whom Pierre knew came up to him, and he had not time to reply to all the questions about Moscow that were showered upon him, or to listen to all that was told him. The faces all expressed animation and apprehension, but it seemed to Pierre that the cause of the excitement shown in some of these faces lay chiefly in questions of personal success; his mind, however, was occupied by the different expression he saw on other faces—an expression that spoke not of personal matters but of the universal questions of life and death. Kutúzov noticed Pierre's figure and the group gathered round him.

"Call him to me," said Kutúzov.

An adjutant told Pierre of his Serene Highness' wish, and Pierre went toward Kutúzov's bench. But a militiaman got there before him. It was Dólokhov.

"How did that fellow get here?" asked Pierre.

"He's a creature that wriggles in anywhere!" was the answer. "He has been degraded, you know. Now he wants to bob up again. He's been proposing some scheme or other and has crawled into the enemy's picket line at night.... He's a brave fellow."

Pierre took off his hat and bowed respectfully to Kutúzov.

"I concluded that if I reported to your Serene Highness you might send me away or say that you knew what I was reporting, but then I shouldn't lose anything..." Dólokhov was saying.

"Yes, yes."

"But if I were right, I should be rendering a service to my Fatherland for which I am ready to die."

"Yes, yes."

"And should your Serene Highness require a man who will not spare his skin, please think of me.... Perhaps I may prove useful to your Serene Highness."

"Yes... Yes..." Kutúzov repeated, his laughing eye narrowing more and more as he looked at Pierre.

Just then Borís, with his courtierlike adroitness, stepped up to Pierre's side near Kutúzov and in a most natural manner, without raising his voice, said to Pierre, as though continuing an interrupted conversation:

"The militia have put on clean white shirts to be ready to die. What heroism, Count!"

Borís evidently said this to Pierre in order to be overheard by his Serene Highness. He knew Kutúzov's attention would be caught by those words, and so it was.

"What are you saying about the militia?" he asked Borís.

"Preparing for tomorrow, your Serene Highness—for death— they have put on clean shirts."

"Ah... a wonderful, a matchless people!" said Kutúzov; and he closed his eyes and swayed his head. "A matchless people!" he repeated with a sigh.

"So you want to smell gunpowder?" he said to Pierre. "Yes, it's a pleasant smell. I have the honor to be one of your wife's adorers. Is she well? My quarters are at your service."

And as often happens with old people, Kutúzov began looking about absent-mindedly as if forgetting all he wanted to say or do.

Then, evidently remembering what he wanted, he beckoned to Andrew Kaysárov, his adjutant's brother.

"Those verses... those verses of Márin's... how do they go, eh? Those he wrote about Gerákov: 'Lectures for the corps inditing'... Recite them, recite them!" said he, evidently preparing to laugh.

Kaysárov recited.... Kutúzov smilingly nodded his head to the rhythm of the verses.

When Pierre had left Kutúzov, Dólokhov came up to him and took his hand.

"I am very glad to meet you here, Count," he said aloud, regardless of the presence of strangers and in a particularly resolute and solemn tone. "On the eve of a day when God alone knows who of us is fated to survive, I am glad of this opportunity to tell you that I regret the misunderstandings that occurred between us and should wish you not to have any ill feeling for me. I beg you to forgive me."

Pierre looked at Dólokhov with a smile, not knowing what to say to him. With tears in his eyes Dólokhov embraced Pierre and kissed him.

Borís said a few words to his general, and Count Bennigsen turned to Pierre and proposed that he should ride with him along the line.

"It will interest you," said he.

"Yes, very much," replied Pierre.

Half an hour later Kutúzov left for Tatárinova, and Bennigsen and his suite, with Pierre among them, set out on their ride along the line.

CHAPTER XXIII

From Górki, Bennigsen descended the highroad to the bridge which, when they had looked at it from the hill, the officer had pointed out as being the center of our position and where rows of fragrant new-mown hay lay by the riverside. They rode across that bridge into the village of Borodinó and thence turned to the left, passing an enormous number of troops and guns, and came to a high knoll where militiamen were digging. This was the redoubt, as yet unnamed, which afterwards became known as the Raévski Redoubt, or the Knoll Battery, but Pierre paid no special attention to it. He did not know that it would become more memorable to him than any other spot on the plain of Borodinó.

They then crossed the hollow to Semënovsk, where the soldiers were dragging away the last logs from the huts and barns. Then they rode downhill and uphill, across a ryefield trodden and beaten down as if by hail, following a track freshly made by the artillery over the furrows of the plowed land, and reached some *flèches* * which were still being dug.

* A kind of entrenchment.

At the *flèches* Bennigsen stopped and began looking at the Shevárdino Redoubt opposite, which had been ours the day before and where several horsemen could be descried. The officers said that either Napoleon or Murat was there, and they all gazed eagerly at this little group of horsemen. Pierre also looked at them, trying to guess which of the scarcely discernible figures was Napoleon. At last those mounted men rode away from the mound and disappeared.

Bennigsen spoke to a general who approached him, and began explaining the whole position of our troops. Pierre listened to him, straining each faculty to understand the essential points of the impending battle, but was mortified to feel that his mental capacity was inadequate for the task. He could make nothing of it. Bennigsen stopped speaking and, noticing that Pierre was listening, suddenly said to him:

"I don't think this interests you?"

"On the contrary it's very interesting!" replied Pierre not quite truthfully.

From the *flèches* they rode still farther to the left, along a road winding through a thick, low-growing birch wood. In the middle of the wood a brown hare with white feet sprang out and, scared by the tramp of the many horses, grew so confused that it leaped along the road in front of them for some time, arousing general attention and laughter, and only when several voices shouted at it did it dart to one side and disappear in the thicket. After going through the wood for about a mile and a half they came out on a glade where troops of Túchkov's corps were stationed to defend the left flank.

Here, at the extreme left flank, Bennigsen talked a great deal and with much heat, and, as it seemed to Pierre, gave orders of great military importance. In front of Túchkov's troops was some high ground not occupied by troops. Bennigsen loudly criticized this mistake, saying that it was madness to leave a height which commanded the country around unoccupied and to place troops below it. Some of the generals expressed the same opinion. One in particular declared with martial heat that they were put there to be slaughtered. Bennigsen on his own authority ordered the troops to occupy the high ground. This disposition on the left flank increased Pierre's doubt of his own capacity to understand military matters. Listening to Bennigsen and the generals criticizing the position of the troops behind the hill, he quite understood them and shared their opinion, but for that very reason he could not understand how the man who put them there behind the hill could have made so gross and palpable a blunder.

Pierre did not know that these troops were not, as Bennigsen supposed, put there to defend the position, but were in a concealed position as an ambush, that they should not be seen and might be able to strike an approaching enemy unexpectedly. Bennigsen did not know this and moved the troops forward according to his own ideas without mentioning the matter to the commander in chief.

CHAPTER XXIV

O n that bright evening of August 25, Prince Andrew lay leaning on his elbow in a broken-down shed in the village of Knyazkóvo at the further end of his regiment's encampment. Through a gap in the broken wall he could see, beside the wooden fence, a row of thirty-year-old birches with their lower branches lopped off, a field on which shocks of oats were standing, and some bushes near which rose the smoke of campfires—the soldiers' kitchens.

Narrow and burdensome and useless to anyone as his life now seemed to him, Prince Andrew on the eve of battle felt agitated and irritable as he had done seven years before at Austerlitz.

He had received and given the orders for next day's battle and had nothing more to do. But his thoughts—the simplest, clearest, and therefore most terrible thoughts—would give him no peace. He knew that tomorrow's battle would be the most terrible of all he had taken part in, and for the first time in his life the possibility of death presented itself to him—not in relation to any worldly matter or with reference to its effect on others, but simply in relation to himself, to his own soul—vividly, plainly, terribly, and almost as a certainty. And from the height of this perception all that had previously tormented and preoccupied him suddenly became illumined by a cold white light without shadows, without perspective, without distinction of outline. All life appeared to him like magic-lantern pictures at which he had long been gazing by artificial light through a glass. Now he suddenly saw those badly daubed pictures in clear daylight and without a glass. "Yes, yes! There they are, those false images that agitated, enraptured, and tormented me," said he to himself, passing in review the principal pictures of the magic lantern of life and regarding them now in the cold white daylight of his clear perception of death. "There they are, those rudely painted figures that once seemed splendid and mysterious. Glory, the good of society, love of a woman, the Fatherland itself—how important these pictures appeared to me, with what profound meaning they seemed to be filled! And it is all so simple, pale, and crude in the cold white light of this morning which I feel is dawning for me." The three great sorrows of his life held his attention in particular: his love for a woman, his father's death, and the French invasion which had overrun half Russia. "Love... that little girl who seemed to me brimming over with mystic forces! Yes, indeed, I loved her. I made romantic plans of love and happiness with her! Oh, what a boy I was!" he said aloud bitterly. "Ah me! I believed in some ideal love which was to keep her faithful to me for the whole year of my absence! Like the gentle dove in the fable she was to pine apart from me.... But it was much simpler really.... It was all very simple and horrible."

"When my father built Bald Hills he thought the place was his: his land, his air, his peasants. But Napoleon came and swept him aside, unconscious of his existence, as he might brush a chip from his path, and his Bald Hills and his whole life fell to pieces. Princess Mary says it is a trial sent from above. What is the trial for, when he is not here and will never return? He is not here! For whom then is the trial intended? The Fatherland, the destruction of Moscow! And tomorrow I shall be killed, perhaps not even by a Frenchman but by one of our own men, by a soldier discharging a musket close to my ear as one of them did yesterday, and the French will come and take me by head and heels and fling me into a hole that I may not stink under their noses, and new conditions of life will arise, which will seem quite ordinary to others and about which I shall know nothing. I shall not exist...."

He looked at the row of birches shining in the sunshine, with their motionless green and yellow foliage and white bark. "To die... to be killed tomorrow... That I should not exist... That all this should still be, but no me...."

And the birches with their light and shade, the curly clouds, the smoke of the campfires, and all that was around him changed and seemed terrible and menacing. A cold shiver ran down his spine. He rose quickly, went out of the shed, and began to walk about.

After he had returned, voices were heard outside the shed. "Who's that?" he cried.

The red-nosed Captain Timókhin, formerly Dólokhov's squadron commander, but now from lack of officers a battalion commander, shyly entered the shed followed by an adjutant and the regimental paymaster.

Prince Andrew rose hastily, listened to the business they had come about, gave them some further instructions, and was about to dismiss them when he heard a familiar, lisping, voice behind the shed.

"Devil take it!" said the voice of a man stumbling over something.

Prince Andrew looked out of the shed and saw Pierre, who had tripped over a pole on the ground and had nearly fallen, coming his way. It was unpleasant to Prince Andrew to meet people of his own set in general, and Pierre especially, for he reminded him of all the painful moments of his last visit to Moscow.

"You? What a surprise!" said he. "What brings you here? This is unexpected!"

As he said this his eyes and face expressed more than coldness— they expressed hostility, which Pierre noticed at once. He had approached the shed full of animation, but on seeing Prince Andrew's face he felt constrained and ill at ease.

"I have come... simply... you know... come... it interests me," said Pierre, who had so often that day senselessly repeated that word "interesting." "I wish to see the battle."

"Oh yes, and what do the Masonic brothers say about war? How would they stop it?" said Prince Andrew sarcastically. "Well, and how's Moscow? And my people? Have they reached Moscow at last?" he asked seriously.

"Yes, they have. Julie Drubetskáya told me so. I went to see them, but missed them. They have gone to your estate near Moscow."

CHAPTER XXV

The officers were about to take leave, but Prince Andrew, apparently reluctant to be left alone with his friend, asked them to stay and have tea. Seats were brought in and so was the tea. The officers gazed with surprise at Pierre's huge stout figure and listened to his talk of Moscow and the position of our army, round which he had ridden. Prince Andrew remained silent, and his expression was so forbidding that Pierre addressed his remarks chiefly to the good-natured battalion commander.

"So you understand the whole position of our troops?" Prince Andrew interrupted him.

"Yes—that is, how do you mean?" said Pierre. "Not being a military man I can't say I have understood it fully, but I understand the general position."

"Well, then, you know more than anyone else, be it who it may," said Prince Andrew.

"Oh!" said Pierre, looking over his spectacles in perplexity at Prince Andrew. "Well, and what do you think of Kutúzov's appointment?" he asked.

"I was very glad of his appointment, that's all I know," replied Prince Andrew.

"And tell me your opinion of Barclay de Tolly. In Moscow they are saying heaven knows what about him.... What do you think of him?"

"Ask them," replied Prince Andrew, indicating the officers.

Pierre looked at Timókhin with the condescendingly interrogative smile with which everybody involuntarily addressed that officer.

"We see light again, since his Serenity has been appointed, your excellency," said Timókhin timidly, and continually turning to glance at his colonel.

"Why so?" asked Pierre.

"Well, to mention only firewood and fodder, let me inform you. Why, when we were retreating from Sventsyáni we dare not touch a stick or a wisp of hay or anything. You see, we were going away, so *he* would get it all; wasn't it so, your excellency?" and again Timókhin turned to the prince. "But we daren't. In our regiment two officers were court-martialed for that kind of thing. But when his Serenity took command everything became straightforward. Now we see light...."

"Then why was it forbidden?"

Timókhin looked about in confusion, not knowing what or how to answer such a question. Pierre put the same question to Prince Andrew.

"Why, so as not to lay waste the country we were abandoning to the enemy," said Prince Andrew with venomous irony. "It is very sound: one can't permit the land to be pillaged and accustom the troops to marauding. At Smolénsk too he judged correctly that the French might outflank us, as they had larger forces. But he could not understand this," cried Prince Andrew in a shrill voice that seemed to escape him involuntarily: "he could not understand that there, for the first time, we were fighting for Russian soil, and that there was a spirit in the men such as I had never seen before, that we had held the French for two days, and that that success had increased our strength tenfold. He ordered us to retreat, and all our efforts and losses went for nothing. He had no thought of betraying us, he tried to do the best he could, he thought out everything, and that is why he is unsuitable. He is unsuitable now, just because he plans out everything very thoroughly and accurately as every German has to. How can I explain?... Well, say your father has a German valet, and he is a splendid valet and satisfies your father's requirements better than you could, then it's all right to let him serve. But if your father is mortally sick you'll send the valet away and attend to your father with your own unpracticed, awkward hands, and will soothe him better than a skilled man who is a stranger could. So it has been with Barclay. While Russia was well, a foreigner could serve her and be a splendid minister; but as soon as she is in danger she needs one of her own kin. But in your Club they have been making him out a traitor! They slander him as a traitor, and the only result will be that afterwards, ashamed of their false accusations, they will make him out a hero or a genius instead of a traitor, and that will be still more unjust. He is an honest and very punctilious German."

"And they say he's a skillful commander," rejoined Pierre.

"I don't understand what is meant by 'a skillful commander,'" replied Prince Andrew ironically.

"A skillful commander?" replied Pierre. "Why, one who foresees all contingencies... and foresees the adversary's intentions."

"But that's impossible," said Prince Andrew as if it were a matter settled long ago.

Pierre looked at him in surprise.

"And yet they say that war is like a game of chess?" he remarked.

"Yes," replied Prince Andrew, "but with this little difference, that in chess you may think over each move as long as you please and are not limited for time, and with this difference too, that a knight is always stronger than a pawn, and two pawns are always stronger than one, while in war a battalion is sometimes stronger than a division and sometimes weaker than a company. The relative strength of bodies of troops can never be known to anyone. Believe me," he went on, "if things depended on arrangements made by the staff, I should be there making arrangements, but instead of that I have the honor to serve here in the regiment with these gentlemen, and I consider that on us tomorrow's battle will depend and not on those others.... Success never depends, and never will depend, on position, or equipment, or even on numbers, and least of all on position."

"But on what then?"

"On the feeling that is in me and in him," he pointed to Timókhin, "and in each soldier."

Prince Andrew glanced at Timókhin, who looked at his commander in alarm and bewilderment. In contrast to his former reticent taciturnity Prince Andrew now seemed excited. He could apparently not refrain from expressing the thoughts that had suddenly occurred to him.

"A battle is won by those who firmly resolve to win it! Why did we lose the battle at Austerlitz? The French losses were almost equal to ours, but very early we said to ourselves that we were losing the battle, and we did lose it. And we said so because we had nothing to fight for there, we wanted to get away from the battlefield as soon as we could. 'We've lost, so let us run,' and we ran. If we had not said that till the evening, heaven knows what might not have happened. But tomorrow we shan't say it! You talk about our position, the left flank weak and the right flank too extended," he went on. "That's all nonsense, there's nothing of the kind. But what awaits us tomorrow? A hundred million most diverse chances which will be decided on the instant by the fact that our men or theirs run or do not run, and that this man or that man is killed, but all that is being done at present is only play. The fact is that those men with whom you have ridden round the position not only do not help matters, but hinder. They are only concerned with their own petty interests."

"At such a moment?" said Pierre reproachfully.

"*At such a moment!*" Prince Andrew repeated. "To them it is only a moment affording opportunities to undermine a rival and obtain an extra cross or ribbon. For me tomorrow means this: a Russian army of a hundred thousand and a French army of a hundred thousand have met to fight, and the thing is that these two hundred thousand men *will* fight and the side that fights more fiercely and spares itself least will win. And if you like I will tell you that whatever happens and whatever muddles those at the top may make, we shall win tomorrow's battle. Tomorrow, happen what may, we shall win!"

"There now, your excellency! That's the truth, the real truth," said Timókhin. "Who would spare himself now? The soldiers in my battalion, believe me, wouldn't drink their vodka! 'It's not the day for that!' they say."

All were silent. The officers rose. Prince Andrew went out of the shed with them, giving final orders to the adjutant. After they had gone Pierre approached Prince Andrew and was about to start a conversation when they heard the clatter of three horses' hoofs on the road not far from the shed, and looking in that direction Prince

Andrew recognized Wolzogen and Clausewitz accompanied by a Cossack. They rode close by continuing to converse, and Prince Andrew involuntarily heard these words:

"Der Krieg muss in Raumverlegtwerden. Der Ansichtkann ich nichtgenugPreisgeben," * said one of them.

* "The war must be extended widely. I cannot sufficiently commend that view."

"Oh, ja," said the other, *"der Zweckistnur den Feindzuschwächen, so kann man gewissnicht den Verlust der Privat-Personen in Achtung nehmen."**

* "Oh, yes, the only aim is to weaken the enemy, so of course one cannot take into account the loss of private individuals."

"Oh, no," agreed the other.

"Extend widely!" said Prince Andrew with an angry snort, when they had ridden past. "In that 'extend' were my father, son, and sister, at Bald Hills. That's all the same to him! That's what I was saying to you—those German gentlemen won't win the battle tomorrow but will only make all the mess they can, because they have nothing in their German heads but theories not worth an empty eggshell and haven't in their hearts the one thing needed tomorrow—that which Timókhin has. They have yielded up all Europe to *him*, and have now come to teach us. Fine teachers!" and again his voice grew shrill.

"So you think we shall win tomorrow's battle?" asked Pierre.

"Yes, yes," answered Prince Andrew absently. "One thing I would do if I had the power," he began again, "I would not take prisoners. Why take prisoners? It's chivalry! The French have destroyed my home and are on their way to destroy Moscow, they have outraged and are outraging me every moment. They are my enemies. In my opinion they are all criminals. And so thinks Timókhin and the whole army. They should be executed! Since they are my foes they cannot be my friends, whatever may have been said at Tilsit."

"Yes, yes," muttered Pierre, looking with shining eyes at Prince Andrew. "I quite agree with you!"

The question that had perturbed Pierre on the Mozháysk hill and all that day now seemed to him quite clear and completely solved. He now understood the whole meaning and importance of this war and of the impending battle. All he had seen that day, all the significant and stern expressions on the faces he had seen in passing, were lit up for him by a new light. He understood that latent heat (as they say in physics) of patriotism which was present in all these men he had seen, and this explained to him why they all prepared for death calmly, and as it were lightheartedly.

"Not take prisoners," Prince Andrew continued: "That by itself would quite change the whole war and make it less cruel. As it is we have played at war—that's what's vile! We play at magnanimity and all that stuff. Such magnanimity and sensibility are like the magnanimity and sensibility of a lady who faints when she sees a calf being killed: she is so kindhearted that she can't look at blood, but enjoys eating the calf served up with sauce. They talk to us of the rules of war, of chivalry, of flags of truce, of mercy to the unfortunate and so on. It's all rubbish! I saw chivalry and flags of truce in 1805; they humbugged us and we humbugged them. They plunder other people's houses, issue false paper money, and worst of all they kill my children and my father, and then talk of rules of war and magnanimity to foes! Take no prisoners, but kill and be killed! He who has come to this as I have through the same sufferings..."

Prince Andrew, who had thought it was all the same to him whether or not Moscow was taken as Smolénsk had been, was suddenly checked in his speech by an unexpected cramp in his throat. He paced up and down a few times in silence, but his eyes glittered feverishly and his lips quivered as he began speaking.

"If there was none of this magnanimity in war, we should go to war only when it was worth while going to certain death, as now. Then there would not be war because Paul Ivánovich had offended Michael Ivánovich. And when there was a war, like this one, it would be war! And then the determination of the troops would be quite different. Then all these Westphalians and Hessians whom Napoleon is leading would not follow him into Russia, and we should not go to fight in Austria and Prussia without knowing why. War is not courtesy but the most horrible thing in life; and we ought to understand that and not play at war. We ought to accept this terrible necessity sternly and seriously. It all lies in that: get rid of falsehood and let war be war and not a game. As it is now, war is the favorite pastime of the idle and frivolous. The military calling is the most highly honored.

"But what is war? What is needed for success in warfare? What are the habits of the military? The aim of war is murder; the methods of war are spying, treachery, and their encouragement, the ruin of a country's inhabitants, robbing them or stealing to provision the army, and fraud and falsehood termed military craft. The habits of the military class are the absence of freedom, that is, discipline, idleness, ignorance, cruelty, debauchery, and drunkenness. And in spite of all this it is the highest class, respected by everyone. All the kings, except the Chinese, wear military uniforms, and he who kills most people receives the highest rewards.

"They meet, as we shall meet tomorrow, to murder one another; they kill and maim tens of thousands, and then have thanksgiving services for having killed so many people (they even exaggerate the number), and they announce a victory, supposing that the more people they have killed the greater their achievement. How does God above look at them and hear them?" exclaimed Prince Andrew in a shrill, piercing voice. "Ah, my friend, it has of late become hard for me to live. I see that I have begun to understand too much. And it doesn't do for man to taste of the tree of knowledge of good and evil.... Ah, well, it's not for long!" he added.

"However, you're sleepy, and it's time for me to sleep. Go back to Górki!" said Prince Andrew suddenly.

"Oh no!" Pierre replied, looking at Prince Andrew with frightened, compassionate eyes.

"Go, go! Before a battle one must have one's sleep out," repeated Prince Andrew.

He came quickly up to Pierre and embraced and kissed him. "Good-by, be off!" he shouted. "Whether we meet again or not..." and turning away hurriedly he entered the shed.

It was already dark, and Pierre could not make out whether the expression of Prince Andrew's face was angry or tender.

For some time he stood in silence considering whether he should follow him or go away. "No, he does not want it!" Pierre concluded. "And I know that this is our last meeting!" He sighed deeply and rode back to Górki.

On re-entering the shed Prince Andrew lay down on a rug, but he could not sleep.

He closed his eyes. One picture succeeded another in his imagination. On one of them he dwelt long and joyfully. He vividly recalled an evening in Petersburg. Natásha with animated and excited face was telling him how she had gone to look for mushrooms the previous summer and had lost her way in the big forest. She incoherently described the depths of the forest, her feelings, and a talk with a beekeeper she met, and constantly interrupted her story to say: "No, I can't! I'm not telling it right; no, you don't understand," though he encouraged her by saying that he did understand, and he really had understood all she wanted to say. But Natásha was not satisfied with her own words: she felt that they did not convey the passionately poetic feeling she had experienced that day and wished to convey. "He was such a delightful old man, and it was so dark in the forest... and he had such kind... No, I can't describe it," she had said, flushed and excited. Prince Andrew smiled now the same happy smile as then when he had looked into her eyes. "I understood her," he thought. "I not only understood her, but it was just that inner, spiritual force, that sincerity, that frankness of soul—that very soul of hers which seemed to be fettered by her body—it was that soul I loved in her... loved so strongly and happily..." and suddenly he remembered how his love had ended. "*He* did not need anything of that kind. *He* neither saw nor understood anything of the sort. He only saw in her a pretty and *fresh* young girl, with whom he did not deign to unite his fate. And I?... and he is still alive and gay!"

Prince Andrew jumped up as if someone had burned him, and again began pacing up and down in front of the shed.

CHAPTER XXVI

O n August 25, the eve of the battle of Borodinó, M. de Beausset, prefect of the French Emperor's palace, arrived at Napoleon's quarters at Valúevo with Colonel Fabvier, the former from Paris and the latter from Madrid.

Donning his court uniform, M. de Beausset ordered a box he had brought for the Emperor to be carried before him and entered the first compartment of Napoleon's tent, where he began opening the box while conversing with Napoleon's aides-de-camp who surrounded him.

Fabvier, not entering the tent, remained at the entrance talking to some generals of his acquaintance.

The Emperor Napoleon had not yet left his bedroom and was finishing his toilet. Slightly snorting and grunting, he presented now his back and now his plump hairy chest to the brush with which his valet was rubbing him down. Another valet, with his finger over the mouth of a bottle, was sprinkling Eau de Cologne on the Emperor's pampered body with an expression which seemed to say that he alone knew where and how much Eau de Cologne should be sprinkled. Napoleon's short hair was wet and matted on the forehead, but his face, though puffy and yellow, expressed physical satisfaction. "Go on, harder, go on!" he muttered to the valet who was rubbing him, slightly twitching and grunting. An aide-de-camp, who had entered the bedroom to report to the Emperor the number of prisoners taken in yesterday's action, was standing by the door after delivering his message, awaiting permission to withdraw. Napoleon, frowning, looked at him from under his brows.

"No prisoners!" said he, repeating the aide-de-camp's words. "They are forcing us to exterminate them. So much the worse for the Russian army.... Go on... harder, harder!" he muttered, hunching his back and presenting his fat shoulders.

"All right. Let Monsieur de Beausset enter, and Fabvier too," he said, nodding to the aide-de-camp.

"Yes, sire," and the aide-de-camp disappeared through the door of the tent.

Two valets rapidly dressed His Majesty, and wearing the blue uniform of the Guards he went with firm quick steps to the reception room.

De Beausset's hands meanwhile were busily engaged arranging the present he had brought from the Empress, on two chairs directly in front of the entrance. But Napoleon had dressed and come out with such unexpected rapidity that he had not time to finish arranging the surprise.

Napoleon noticed at once what they were about and guessed that they were not ready. He did not wish to deprive them of the pleasure of giving him a surprise, so he pretended not to see de Beausset and called Fabvier to him, listening silently and with a stern frown to what Fabvier told him of the heroism and devotion of his troops fighting at Salamanca, at the other end of Europe, with but one thought—to be worthy of their Emperor—and but one fear— to fail to please him. The result of that battle had been deplorable. Napoleon made ironic remarks during Fabvier's account, as if he had not expected that matters could go otherwise in his absence.

"I must make up for that in Moscow," said Napoleon. "I'll see you later," he added, and summoned de Beausset, who by that time had prepared the surprise, having placed something on the chairs and covered it with a cloth.

De Beausset bowed low, with that courtly French bow which only the old retainers of the Bourbons knew how to make, and approached him, presenting an envelope.

Napoleon turned to him gaily and pulled his ear.

"You have hurried here. I am very glad. Well, what is Paris saying?" he asked, suddenly changing his former stern expression for a most cordial tone.

"Sire, all Paris regrets your absence," replied de Beausset as was proper.

But though Napoleon knew that de Beausset had to say something of this kind, and though in his lucid moments he knew it was untrue, he was pleased to hear it from him. Again he honored him by touching his ear.

"I am very sorry to have made you travel so far," said he.

"Sire, I expected nothing less than to find you at the gates of Moscow," replied de Beausset.

Napoleon smiled and, lifting his head absent-mindedly, glanced to the right. An aide-de-camp approached with gliding steps and offered him a gold snuffbox, which he took.

"Yes, it has happened luckily for you," he said, raising the open snuffbox to his nose. "You are fond of travel, and in three days you will see Moscow. You surely did not expect to see that Asiatic capital. You will have a pleasant journey."

De Beausset bowed gratefully at this regard for his taste for travel (of which he had not till then been aware).

"Ha, what's this?" asked Napoleon, noticing that all the courtiers were looking at something concealed under a cloth.

With courtly adroitness de Beausset half turned and without turning his back to the Emperor retired two steps, twitching off the cloth at the same time, and said:

"A present to Your Majesty from the Empress."

It was a portrait, painted in bright colors by Gérard, of the son borne to Napoleon by the daughter of the Emperor of Austria, the boy whom for some reason everyone called "The King of Rome."

A very pretty curly-headed boy with a look of the Christ in the Sistine Madonna was depicted playing at stick and ball. The ball represented the terrestrial globe and the stick in his other hand a scepter.

Though it was not clear what the artist meant to express by depicting the so-called King of Rome spiking the earth with a stick, the allegory apparently seemed to Napoleon, as it had done to all who had seen it in Paris, quite clear and very pleasing.

"The King of Rome!" he said, pointing to the portrait with a graceful gesture. "Admirable!"

With the natural capacity of an Italian for changing the expression of his face at will, he drew nearer to the portrait and assumed a look of pensive tenderness. He felt that what he now said and did would be historical, and it seemed to him that it would now be best for him—whose grandeur enabled his son to play stick and ball with the terrestrial globe—to show, in contrast to that grandeur, the simplest paternal tenderness. His eyes grew dim, he moved forward, glanced round at a chair (which seemed to place itself under him), and sat down on it before the portrait. At a single gesture from him everyone went out on tiptoe, leaving the great man to himself and his emotion.

Having sat still for a while he touched—himself not knowing why—the thick spot of paint representing the highest light in the portrait, rose, and recalled de Beausset and the officer on duty. He ordered the portrait to be carried outside his tent, that the Old Guard, stationed round it, might not be deprived of the pleasure of seeing the King of Rome, the son and heir of their adored monarch.

And while he was doing M. de Beausset the honor of breakfasting with him, they heard, as Napoleon had anticipated, the rapturous cries of the officers and men of the Old Guard who had run up to see the portrait.

"Vivel'Empereur! Vive le roi de Rome! Vivel'Empereur!" came those ecstatic cries.

After breakfast Napoleon in de Beausset's presence dictated his order of the day to the army.

"Short and energetic!" he remarked when he had read over the proclamation which he had dictated straight off without corrections. It ran:

Soldiers! This is the battle you have so longed for. Victory depends on you. It is essential for us; it will give us all we need: comfortable quarters and a speedy return to our country. Behave as you did at Austerlitz, Friedland, Vítebsk, and Smolénsk. Let our remotest posterity recall your achievements this day with pride. Let it be said of each of you: "He was in the great battle before Moscow!"

"Before Moscow!" repeated Napoleon, and inviting M. de Beausset, who was so fond of travel, to accompany him on his ride, he went out of the tent to where the horses stood saddled.

"Your Majesty is too kind!" replied de Beausset to the invitation to accompany the Emperor; he wanted to sleep, did not know how to ride and was afraid of doing so.

But Napoleon nodded to the traveler, and de Beausset had to mount. When Napoleon came out of the tent the shouting of the Guards before his son's portrait grew still louder. Napoleon frowned.

"Take him away!" he said, pointing with a gracefully majestic gesture to the portrait. "It is too soon for him to see a field of battle."

De Beausset closed his eyes, bowed his head, and sighed deeply, to indicate how profoundly he valued and comprehended the Emperor's words.

CHAPTER XXVII

On the twenty-fifth of August, so his historians tell us, Napoleon spent the whole day on horseback inspecting the locality, considering plans submitted to him by his marshals, and personally giving commands to his generals.

The original line of the Russian forces along the river Kolochá had been dislocated by the capture of the Shevárdino Redoubt on the twenty-fourth, and part of the line—the left flank—had been drawn back. That part of the line was not entrenched and in front of it the ground was more open and level than elsewhere. It was evident to anyone, military or not, that it was here the French should attack. It would seem that not much consideration was needed to reach this conclusion, nor any particular care or trouble on the part of the Emperor and his marshals, nor was there any need of that special and supreme quality called genius that people are so apt to ascribe to Napoleon; yet the historians who described the event later and the men who then surrounded Napoleon, and he himself, thought otherwise.

Napoleon rode over the plain and surveyed the locality with a profound air and in silence, nodded with approval or shook his head dubiously, and without communicating to the generals around him the profound course of ideas which guided his decisions merely gave them his final conclusions in the form of commands. Having listened to a suggestion from Davout, who was now called Prince d'Eckmühl, to turn the Russian left wing, Napoleon said it should not be done, without explaining why not. To a proposal made by General Campan (who was to attack the *flèches*) to lead his division through the woods, Napoleon agreed, though the so-called Duke of Elchingen (Ney) ventured to remark that a movement through the woods was dangerous and might disorder the division.

Having inspected the country opposite the Shevárdino Redoubt, Napoleon pondered a little in silence and then indicated the spots where two batteries should be set up by the morrow to act against the Russian entrenchments, and the places where, in line with them, the field artillery should be placed.

After giving these and other commands he returned to his tent, and the dispositions for the battle were written down from his dictation.

These dispositions, of which the French historians write with enthusiasm and other historians with profound respect, were as follows:

At dawn the two new batteries established during the night on the plain occupied by the Princed'Eckmühl will open fire on the opposing batteries of the enemy.

At the same time the commander of the artillery of the 1st Corps, General Pernetti, with thirty cannon of Campan's division and all the howitzers of Dessaix's and Friant's divisions, will move forward, open fire, and overwhelm with shellfire the enemy's battery, against which will operate:

24 guns of the artillery of the Guards

30 guns of Campan's division

and 8 guns of Friant's and Dessaix's divisions

—

in all 62 guns.

The commander of the artillery of the 3rd Corps, General Fouché, will place the howitzers of the 3rd and 8th Corps, sixteen in all, on the flanks of the battery that is to bombard the entrenchment on the left, which will have forty guns in all directed against it.

General Sorbier must be ready at the first order to advance with all the howitzers of the Guard's artillery against either one or other of the entrenchments.

During the cannonade Prince Poniatowski is to advance through the wood on the village and turn the enemy's position.

General Campan will move through the wood to seize the first fortification.

After the advance has begun in this manner, orders will be given in accordance with the enemy's movements.

The cannonade on the left flank will begin as soon as the guns of the right wing are heard. The sharpshooters of Morand's division and of the vice-King's division will open a heavy fire on seeing the attack commence on the right wing.

The vice-King will occupy the village and cross by its three bridges, advancing to the same heights as Morand's and Gibrard's divisions, which under his leadership will be directed against the redoubt and come into line with the rest of the forces.

All this must be done in good order (*le tout se fera avec ordre et méthode*) as far as possible retaining troops in reserve.

The Imperial Camp near Mozháysk,

September, 6, 1812.

These dispositions, which are very obscure and confused if one allows oneself to regard the arrangements without religious awe of his genius, related to Napoleon's orders to deal with four points—four different orders. Not one of these was, or could be, carried out.

In the disposition it is said first *that the batteries placed on the spot chosen by Napoleon, with the guns of Pernetti and Fouché; which were to come in line with them, 102 guns in all, were to open fire and shower shells on the Russian* flèches *and redoubts.* This could not be done, as from the spots selected by Napoleon the projectiles did not carry to the Russian works, and those 102 guns shot into the air until the nearest commander, contrary to Napoleon's instructions, moved them forward.

The second order was that *Poniatowski, moving to the village through the wood, should turn the Russian left flank.* This could not be done and was not done, because Poniatowski, advancing on the village through the wood, met Túchkov there barring his way, and could not and did not turn the Russian position.

The third order was: *General Campan will move through the wood to seize the first fortification.* General Campan's division did not seize the first fortification but was driven back, for on emerging from the wood it had to reform under grapeshot, of which Napoleon was unaware.

The fourth order was: *The vice-King will occupy the village* (Borodinó) *and cross by its three bridges, advancing to the same heights as Morand's and Gérard's divisions* (for whose movements no directions are given), *which under his leadership will be directed against the redoubt and come into line with the rest of the forces.*

As far as one can make out, not so much from this unintelligible sentence as from the attempts the vice-King made to execute the orders given him, he was to advance from the left through Borodinó to the redoubt while the divisions of Morand and Gérard were to advance simultaneously from the front.

All this, like the other parts of the disposition, was not and could not be executed. After passing through Borodinó the vice-King was driven back to the Kolochá and could get no farther; while the divisions of Morand and Gérard did not take the redoubt but were driven back, and the redoubt was only taken at the end of the battle by the cavalry (a thing probably unforeseen and not heard of by Napoleon). So not one of the orders in the disposition was, or could be, executed. But in the disposition it is said that, *after the fight has commenced in this manner, orders will be given in accordance with the enemy's movements*, and so it might be supposed that all necessary arrangements would be made by Napoleon during the battle. But this was not and could not be done, for during the whole battle Napoleon was so far away that, as appeared later, he could not know the course of the battle and not one of his orders during the fight could be executed.

CHAPTER XXVIII

M any historians say that the French did not win the battle of
Borodinó because Napoleon had a cold, and that if he had not
had a cold the orders he gave before and during the battle would have
been still more full of genius and Russia would have been lost and
the face of the world have been changed. To historians who believe
that Russia was shaped by the will of one man—Peter the Great—
and that France from a republic became an empire and French armies
went to Russia at the will of one man—Napoleon—to say that Russia
remained a power because Napoleon had a bad cold on the twenty-
fourth of August may seem logical and convincing.

If it had depended on Napoleon's will to fight or not to fight the
battle of Borodinó, and if this or that other arrangement depended on
his will, then evidently a cold affecting the manifestation of his will
might have saved Russia, and consequently the valet who omitted
to bring Napoleon his waterproof boots on the twenty-fourth would
have been the savior of Russia. Along that line of thought such a
deduction is indubitable, as indubitable as the deduction Voltaire
made in jest (without knowing what he was jesting at) when he
saw that the Massacre of St. Bartholomew was due to Charles IX's
stomach being deranged. But to men who do not admit that Russia
was formed by the will of one man, Peter I, or that the French Empire
was formed and the war with Russia begun by the will of one man,
Napoleon, that argument seems not merely untrue and irrational, but
contrary to all human reality. To the question of what causes historic
events another answer presents itself, namely, that the course of
human events is predetermined from on high—depends on the
coincidence of the wills of all who take part in the events, and that a

Napoleon's influence on the course of these events is purely external and fictitious.

Strange as at first glance it may seem to suppose that the Massacre of St. Bartholomew was not due to Charles IX's will, though he gave the order for it and thought it was done as a result of that order; and strange as it may seem to suppose that the slaughter of eighty thousand men at Borodinó was not due to Napoleon's will, though he ordered the commencement and conduct of the battle and thought it was done because he ordered it; strange as these suppositions appear, yet human dignity—which tells me that each of us is, if not more at least not less a man than the great Napoleon—demands the acceptance of that solution of the question, and historic investigation abundantly confirms it.

At the battle of Borodinó Napoleon shot at no one and killed no one. That was all done by the soldiers. Therefore it was not he who killed people.

The French soldiers went to kill and be killed at the battle of Borodinó not because of Napoleon's orders but by their own volition. The whole army—French, Italian, German, Polish, and Dutch—hungry, ragged, and weary of the campaign, felt at the sight of an army blocking their road to Moscow that the wine was drawn and must be drunk. Had Napoleon then forbidden them to fight the Russians, they would have killed him and have proceeded to fight the Russians because it was inevitable.

When they heard Napoleon's proclamation offering them, as compensation for mutilation and death, the words of posterity about their having been in the battle before Moscow, they cried *"Vivel'Empereur!"* just as they had cried *"Vivel'Empereur!"* at the sight of the portrait of the boy piercing the terrestrial globe with a toy stick, and just as they would have cried *"Vivel'Empereur!"* at any nonsense that might be told them. There was nothing left for them to do but cry *"Vivel'Empereur!"* and go to fight, in order to get food and rest as conquerors in Moscow. So it was not because of Napoleon's commands that they killed their fellow men.

And it was not Napoleon who directed the course of the battle, for none of his orders were executed and during the battle he did not know what was going on before him. So the way in which these people killed one another was not decided by Napoleon's will but occurred independently of him, in accord with the will of hundreds of thousands of people who took part in the common action. It *only seemed* to Napoleon that it all took place by his will. And so the question whether he had or had not a cold has no more historic interest than the cold of the least of the transport soldiers.

Moreover, the assertion made by various writers that his cold was the cause of his dispositions not being as well-planned as on former occasions, and of his orders during the battle not being as good as previously, is quite baseless, which again shows that Napoleon's cold on the twenty-sixth of August was unimportant.

The dispositions cited above are not at all worse, but are even better, than previous dispositions by which he had won victories. His pseudo-orders during the battle were also no worse than formerly, but much the same as usual. These dispositions and orders only seem worse than previous ones because the battle of Borodinó was the first Napoleon did not win. The profoundest and most excellent dispositions and orders seem very bad, and every learned militarist criticizes them with looks of importance, when they relate to a battle that has been lost, and the very worst dispositions and orders seem very good, and serious people fill whole volumes to demonstrate their merits, when they relate to a battle that has been won.

The dispositions drawn up by Weyrother for the battle of Austerlitz were a model of perfection for that kind of composition, but still they were criticized—criticized for their very perfection, for their excessive minuteness.

Napoleon at the battle of Borodinó fulfilled his office as representative of authority as well as, and even better than, at other battles. He did nothing harmful to the progress of the battle; he inclined to the most reasonable opinions, he made no confusion, did not contradict himself, did not get frightened or run away from the field of battle, but with his great tact and military experience carried out his role of appearing to command, calmly and with dignity.

CHAPTER XXIX

O n returning from a second inspection of the lines, Napoleon remarked:

"The chessmen are set up, the game will begin tomorrow!"

Having ordered punch and summoned de Beausset, he began to talk to him about Paris and about some changes he meant to make in the Empress' household, surprising the prefect by his memory of minute details relating to the court.

He showed an interest in trifles, joked about de Beausset's love of travel, and chatted carelessly, as a famous, self-confident surgeon who knows his job does when turning up his sleeves and putting on his apron while a patient is being strapped to the operating table. "The matter is in my hands and is clear and definite in my head. When the time comes to set to work I shall do it as no one else could, but now I can jest, and the more I jest and the calmer I am the more tranquil and confident you ought to be, and the more amazed at my genius."

Having finished his second glass of punch, Napoleon went to rest before the serious business which, he considered, awaited him next day. He was so much interested in that task that he was unable to sleep, and in spite of his cold which had grown worse from the dampness of the evening, he went into the large division of the tent at three o'clock in the morning, loudly blowing his nose. He asked whether the Russians had not withdrawn, and was told that the enemy's fires were still in the same places. He nodded approval.

The adjutant in attendance came into the tent.

"Well, Rapp, do you think we shall do good business today?" Napoleon asked him.

"Without doubt, sire," replied Rapp.

Napoleon looked at him.

"Do you remember, sire, what you did me the honor to say at Smolénsk?" continued Rapp. "The wine is drawn and must be drunk."

Napoleon frowned and sat silent for a long time leaning his head on his hand.

"This poor army!" he suddenly remarked. "It has diminished greatly since Smolénsk. Fortune is frankly a courtesan, Rapp. I have always said so and I am beginning to experience it. But the Guards, Rapp, the Guards are intact?" he remarked interrogatively.

"Yes, sire," replied Rapp.

Napoleon took a lozenge, put it in his mouth, and glanced at his watch. He was not sleepy and it was still not nearly morning. It was impossible to give further orders for the sake of killing time, for the orders had all been given and were now being executed.

"Have the biscuits and rice been served out to the regiments of the Guards?" asked Napoleon sternly.

"Yes, sire."

"The rice too?"

Rapp replied that he had given the Emperor's order about the rice, but Napoleon shook his head in dissatisfaction as if not believing that his order had been executed. An attendant came in with punch. Napoleon ordered another glass to be brought for Rapp, and silently sipped his own.

"I have neither taste nor smell," he remarked, sniffing at his glass. "This cold is tiresome. They talk about medicine—what is the good of medicine when it can't cure a cold! Corvisart gave me these lozenges but they don't help at all. What can doctors cure? One can't cure anything. Our body is a machine for living. It is organized for that, it is its nature. Let life go on in it unhindered and let it defend itself, it will do more than if you paralyze it by encumbering it with remedies.

Our body is like a perfect watch that should go for a certain time; the watchmaker cannot open it, he can only adjust it by fumbling, and that blindfold.... Yes, our body is just a machine for living, that is all."

And having entered on the path of definition, of which he was fond, Napoleon suddenly and unexpectedly gave a new one.

"Do you know, Rapp, what military art is?" asked he. "It is the art of being stronger than the enemy at a given moment. That's all."

Rapp made no reply.

"Tomorrow we shall have to deal with Kutúzov!" said Napoleon. "We shall see! Do you remember at Braunau he commanded an army for three weeks and did not once mount a horse to inspect his entrenchments.... We shall see!"

He looked at his watch. It was still only four o'clock. He did not feel sleepy. The punch was finished and there was still nothing to do. He rose, walked to and fro, put on a warm overcoat and a hat, and went out of the tent. The night was dark and damp, a scarcely perceptible moisture was descending from above. Near by, the campfires were dimly burning among the French Guards, and in the distance those of the Russian line shone through the smoke. The weather was calm, and the rustle and tramp of the French troops already beginning to move to take up their positions were clearly audible.

Napoleon walked about in front of his tent, looked at the fires and listened to these sounds, and as he was passing a tall guardsman in a shaggy cap, who was standing sentinel before his tent and had drawn himself up like a black pillar at sight of the Emperor, Napoleon stopped in front of him.

"What year did you enter the service?" he asked with that affectation of military bluntness and geniality with which he always addressed the soldiers.

The man answered the question.

"Ah! One of the old ones! Has your regiment had its rice?"

"It has, Your Majesty."

Napoleon nodded and walked away.

At half-past five Napoleon rode to the village of Shevárdino.

It was growing light, the sky was clearing, only a single cloud lay in the east. The abandoned campfires were burning themselves out in the faint morning light.

On the right a single deep report of a cannon resounded and died away in the prevailing silence. Some minutes passed. A second and a third report shook the air, then a fourth and a fifth boomed solemnly near by on the right.

The first shots had not yet ceased to reverberate before others rang out and yet more were heard mingling with and overtaking one another.

Napoleon with his suite rode up to the Shevárdino Redoubt where he dismounted. The game had begun.

CHAPTER XXX

O n returning to Górki after having seen Prince Andrew, Pierre
ordered his groom to get the horses ready and to call him early
in the morning, and then immediately fell asleep behind a partition in
a corner Borís had given up to him.

Before he was thoroughly awake next morning everybody had
already left the hut. The panes were rattling in the little windows and
his groom was shaking him.

"Your excellency! Your excellency! Your excellency!" he kept
repeating pertinaciously while he shook Pierre by the shoulder
without looking at him, having apparently lost hope of getting him
to wake up.

"What? Has it begun? Is it time?" Pierre asked, waking up.

"Hear the firing," said the groom, a discharged soldier. "All the
gentlemen have gone out, and his Serene Highness himself rode past
long ago."

Pierre dressed hastily and ran out to the porch. Outside all was
bright, fresh, dewy, and cheerful. The sun, just bursting forth from
behind a cloud that had concealed it, was shining, with rays still half
broken by the clouds, over the roofs of the street opposite, on the
dew-besprinkled dust of the road, on the walls of the houses, on
the windows, the fence, and on Pierre's horses standing before the
hut. The roar of guns sounded more distinct outside. An adjutant
accompanied by a Cossack passed by at a sharp trot.

"It's time, Count; it's time!" cried the adjutant.

Telling the groom to follow him with the horses, Pierre went down the street to the knoll from which he had looked at the field of battle the day before. A crowd of military men was assembled there, members of the staff could be heard conversing in French, and Kutúzov'sgray head in a white cap with a red band was visible, his gray nape sunk between his shoulders. He was looking through a field glass down the highroad before him.

Mounting the steps to the knoll Pierre looked at the scene before him, spellbound by beauty. It was the same panorama he had admired from that spot the day before, but now the whole place was full of troops and covered by smoke clouds from the guns, and the slanting rays of the bright sun, rising slightly to the left behind Pierre, cast upon it through the clear morning air penetrating streaks of rosy, golden-tinted light and long dark shadows. The forest at the farthest extremity of the panorama seemed carved in some precious stone of a yellowish-green color; its undulating outline was silhouetted against the horizon and was pierced beyond Valúevo by the Smolénsk highroad crowded with troops. Nearer at hand glittered golden cornfields interspersed with copses. There were troops to be seen everywhere, in front and to the right and left. All this was vivid, majestic, and unexpected; but what impressed Pierre most of all was the view of the battlefield itself, of Borodinó and the hollows on both sides of the Kolochá.

Above the Kolochá, in Borodinó and on both sides of it, especially to the left where the Vóyna flowing between its marshy banks falls into the Kolochá, a mist had spread which seemed to melt, to dissolve, and to become translucent when the brilliant sun appeared and magically colored and outlined everything. The smoke of the guns mingled with this mist, and over the whole expanse and through that mist the rays of the morning sun were reflected, flashing back like lightning from the water, from the dew, and from the bayonets of the troops crowded together by the riverbanks and in Borodinó. A white church could be seen through the mist, and here and there the roofs of huts in Borodinó as well as dense masses of soldiers, or green ammunition chests and ordnance. And all this moved, or seemed to move, as the smoke and mist spread out over the whole space. Just as in the mist-enveloped hollow near Borodinó, so along the entire line outside and above it and especially in the woods and fields to the left, in the valleys and on the summits of the high ground, clouds of powder smoke seemed continually to spring up out of nothing, now singly, now several at a time, some translucent, others dense, which, swelling, growing, rolling, and blending, extended over the whole expanse.

These puffs of smoke and (strange to say) the sound of the firing produced the chief beauty of the spectacle.

"*Puff!*"—suddenly a round compact cloud of smoke was seen merging from violet into gray and milky white, and "*boom!*" came the report a second later.

"*Puff! puff!*"—and two clouds arose pushing one another and blending together; and "*boom, boom!*" came the sounds confirming what the eye had seen.

Pierre glanced round at the first cloud, which he had seen as a round compact ball, and in its place already were balloons of smoke floating to one side, and—"*puff*" (with a pause)—"*puff, puff!*" three and then four more appeared and then from each, with the same interval—"*boom—boom, boom!*" came the fine, firm, precise sounds in reply. It seemed as if those smoke clouds sometimes ran and sometimes stood still while woods, fields, and glittering bayonets ran past them. From the left, over fields and bushes, those large balls of smoke were continually appearing followed by their solemn reports, while nearer still, in the hollows and woods, there burst from the muskets small cloudlets that had no time to become balls, but had their little echoes in just the same way. "*Trakh-ta-ta-takh!*" came the frequent crackle of musketry, but it was irregular and feeble in comparison with the reports of the cannon.

Pierre wished to be there with that smoke, those shining bayonets, that movement, and those sounds. He turned to look at Kutúzov and his suite, to compare his impressions with those of others. They were all looking at the field of battle as he was, and, as it seemed to him, with the same feelings. All their faces were now shining with that latent warmth of feeling Pierre had noticed the day before and had fully understood after his talk with Prince Andrew.

"Go, my dear fellow, go... and Christ be with you!" Kutúzov was saying to a general who stood beside him, not taking his eye from the battlefield.

Having received this order the general passed by Pierre on his way down the knoll.

"To the crossing!" said the general coldly and sternly in reply to one of the staff who asked where he was going.

"I'll go there too, I too!" thought Pierre, and followed the general.

The general mounted a horse a Cossack had brought him. Pierre went to his groom who was holding his horses and, asking which was the quietest, clambered onto it, seized it by the mane, and turning out his toes pressed his heels against its sides and, feeling that his spectacles were slipping off but unable to let go of the mane and reins, he galloped after the general, causing the staff officers to smile as they watched him from the knoll.

CHAPTER XXXI

H aving descended the hill the general after whom Pierre was galloping turned sharply to the left, and Pierre, losing sight of him, galloped in among some ranks of infantry marching ahead of him. He tried to pass either in front of them or to the right or left, but there were soldiers everywhere, all with the same preoccupied expression and busy with some unseen but evidently important task. They all gazed with the same dissatisfied and inquiring expression at this stout man in a white hat, who for some unknown reason threatened to trample them under his horse's hoofs.

"Why ride into the middle of the battalion?" one of them shouted at him.

Another prodded his horse with the butt end of a musket, and Pierre, bending over his saddlebow and hardly able to control his shying horse, galloped ahead of the soldiers where there was a free space.

There was a bridge ahead of him, where other soldiers stood firing. Pierre rode up to them. Without being aware of it he had come to the bridge across the Kolochá between Górki and Borodinó, which the French (having occupied Borodinó) were attacking in the first phase of the battle. Pierre saw that there was a bridge in front of him and that soldiers were doing something on both sides of it and in the meadow, among the rows of new-mown hay which he had taken no notice of amid the smoke of the campfires the day before; but despite the incessant firing going on there he had no idea that this was the field of battle. He did not notice the sound of the bullets whistling from every side, or the projectiles that flew over him, did not see the enemy on the other side of the river, and for a long time did not notice the killed and wounded, though many fell near him. He looked about him with a smile which did not leave his face.

"Why's that fellow in front of the line?" shouted somebody at him again.

"To the left!... Keep to the right!" the men shouted to him.

Pierre went to the right, and unexpectedly encountered one of Raévski's adjutants whom he knew. The adjutant looked angrily at him, evidently also intending to shout at him, but on recognizing him he nodded.

"How have you got here?" he said, and galloped on.

Pierre, feeling out of place there, having nothing to do, and afraid of getting in someone's way again, galloped after the adjutant.

"What's happening here? May I come with you?" he asked.

"One moment, one moment!" replied the adjutant, and riding up to a stout colonel who was standing in the meadow, he gave him some message and then addressed Pierre.

"Why have you come here, Count?" he asked with a smile. "Still inquisitive?"

"Yes, yes," assented Pierre.

But the adjutant turned his horse about and rode on.

"Here it's tolerable," said he, "but with Bagratión on the left flank they're getting it frightfully hot."

"Really?" said Pierre. "Where is that?"

"Come along with me to our knoll. We can get a view from there and in our battery it is still bearable," said the adjutant. "Will you come?"

"Yes, I'll come with you," replied Pierre, looking round for his groom.

It was only now that he noticed wounded men staggering along or being carried on stretchers. On that very meadow he had ridden over the day before, a soldier was lying athwart the rows of scented hay, with his head thrown awkwardly back and his shako off.

"Why haven't they carried him away?" Pierre was about to ask, but seeing the stern expression of the adjutant who was also looking that way, he checked himself.

Pierre did not find his groom and rode along the hollow with the adjutant to Raévski's Redoubt. His horse lagged behind the adjutant's and jolted him at every step.

"You don't seem to be used to riding, Count?" remarked the adjutant.

"No it's not that, but her action seems so jerky," said Pierre in a puzzled tone.

"Why... she's wounded!" said the adjutant. "In the off foreleg above the knee. A bullet, no doubt. I congratulate you, Count, on your baptism of fire!"

Having ridden in the smoke past the Sixth Corps, behind the artillery which had been moved forward and was in action, deafening them with the noise of firing, they came to a small wood. There it was cool and quiet, with a scent of autumn. Pierre and the adjutant dismounted and walked up the hill on foot.

"Is the general here?" asked the adjutant on reaching the knoll.

"He was here a minute ago but has just gone that way," someone told him, pointing to the right.

The adjutant looked at Pierre as if puzzled what to do with him now.

"Don't trouble about me," said Pierre. "I'll go up onto the knoll if I may?"

"Yes, do. You'll see everything from there and it's less dangerous, and I'll come for you."

Pierre went to the battery and the adjutant rode on. They did not meet again, and only much later did Pierre learn that he lost an arm that day.

The knoll to which Pierre ascended was that famous one afterwards known to the Russians as the Knoll Battery or Raévski's Redoubt, and to the French as *la granderedoute, la fatale redoute, la redoute du centre*, around which tens of thousands fell, and which the French regarded as the key to the whole position.

This redoubt consisted of a knoll, on three sides of which trenches had been dug. Within the entrenchment stood ten guns that were being fired through openings in the earthwork.

In line with the knoll on both sides stood other guns which also fired incessantly. A little behind the guns stood infantry. When ascending that knoll Pierre had no notion that this spot, on which small trenches had been dug and from which a few guns were firing, was the most important point of the battle.

On the contrary, just because he happened to be there he thought it one of the least significant parts of the field.

Having reached the knoll, Pierre sat down at one end of a trench surrounding the battery and gazed at what was going on around him with an unconsciously happy smile. Occasionally he rose and walked about the battery still with that same smile, trying not to obstruct the soldiers who were loading, hauling the guns, and continually running past him with bags and charges. The guns of that battery were being fired continually one after another with a deafening roar, enveloping the whole neighborhood in powder smoke.

In contrast with the dread felt by the infantrymen placed in support, here in the battery where a small number of men busy at their work were separated from the rest by a trench, everyone experienced a common and as it were family feeling of animation.

The intrusion of Pierre's nonmilitary figure in a white hat made an unpleasant impression at first. The soldiers looked askance at him with surprise and even alarm as they went past him. The senior artillery officer, a tall, long-legged, pockmarked man, moved over to Pierre as if to see the action of the farthest gun and looked at him with curiosity.

A young round-faced officer, quite a boy still and evidently only just out of the Cadet College, who was zealously commanding the two guns entrusted to him, addressed Pierre sternly.

"Sir," he said, "permit me to ask you to stand aside. You must not be here."

The soldiers shook their heads disapprovingly as they looked at Pierre. But when they had convinced themselves that this man in the white hat was doing no harm, but either sat quietly on the slope of the trench with a shy smile or, politely making way for the soldiers, paced up and down the battery under fire as calmly as if he were on a boulevard, their feeling of hostile distrust gradually began to change into a kindly and bantering sympathy, such as soldiers feel for their dogs, cocks, goats, and in general for the animals that live with the regiment. The men soon accepted Pierre into their family, adopted him, gave him a nickname ("our gentleman"), and made kindly fun of him among themselves.

A shell tore up the earth two paces from Pierre and he looked around with a smile as he brushed from his clothes some earth it had thrown up.

"And how's it you're not afraid, sir, really now?" a red-faced, broad-shouldered soldier asked Pierre, with a grin that disclosed a set of sound, white teeth.

"Are you afraid, then?" said Pierre.

"What else do you expect?" answered the soldier. "She has no mercy, you know! When she comes spluttering down, out go your innards. One can't help being afraid," he said laughing.

Several of the men, with bright kindly faces, stopped beside Pierre. They seemed not to have expected him to talk like anybody else, and the discovery that he did so delighted them.

"It's the business of us soldiers. But in a gentleman it's wonderful! There's a gentleman for you!"

"To your places!" cried the young officer to the men gathered round Pierre.

The young officer was evidently exercising his duties for the first or second time and therefore treated both his superiors and the men with great precision and formality.

The booming cannonade and the fusillade of musketry were growing more intense over the whole field, especially to the left where Bagratión's *flèches* were, but where Pierre was the smoke of the firing made it almost impossible to distinguish anything. Moreover, his whole attention was engrossed by watching the family circle—separated from all else—formed by the men in the battery. His first unconscious feeling of joyful animation produced by the sights and sounds of the battlefield was now replaced by another, especially since he had seen that soldier lying alone in the hayfield. Now, seated on the slope of the trench, he observed the faces of those around him.

By ten o'clock some twenty men had already been carried away from the battery; two guns were smashed and cannon balls fell more and more frequently on the battery and spent bullets buzzed and whistled around. But the men in the battery seemed not to notice this, and merry voices and jokes were heard on all sides.

"A live one!" shouted a man as a whistling shell approached.

"Not this way! To the infantry!" added another with loud laughter, seeing the shell fly past and fall into the ranks of the supports.

"Are you bowing to a friend, eh?" remarked another, chaffing a peasant who ducked low as a cannon ball flew over.

Several soldiers gathered by the wall of the trench, looking out to see what was happening in front.

"They've withdrawn the front line, it has retired," said they, pointing over the earthwork.

"Mind your own business," an old sergeant shouted at them. "If they've retired it's because there's work for them to do farther back."

And the sergeant, taking one of the men by the shoulders, gave him a shove with his knee. This was followed by a burst of laughter.

"To the fifth gun, wheel it up!" came shouts from one side.

"Now then, all together, like bargees!" rose the merry voices of those who were moving the gun.

"Oh, she nearly knocked our gentleman's hat off!" cried the red-faced humorist, showing his teeth chaffing Pierre. "Awkward baggage!" he added reproachfully to a cannon ball that struck a cannon wheel and a man's leg.

"Now then, you foxes!" said another, laughing at some militiamen who, stooping low, entered the battery to carry away the wounded man.

"So this gruel isn't to your taste? Oh, you crows! You're scared!" they shouted at the militiamen who stood hesitating before the man whose leg had been torn off.

"There, lads... oh, oh!" they mimicked the peasants, "they don't like it at all!"

Pierre noticed that after every ball that hit the redoubt, and after every loss, the liveliness increased more and more.

As the flames of the fire hidden within come more and more vividly and rapidly from an approaching thundercloud, so, as if in opposition to what was taking place, the lightning of hidden fire growing more and more intense glowed in the faces of these men.

Pierre did not look out at the battlefield and was not concerned to know what was happening there; he was entirely absorbed in watching this fire which burned ever more brightly and which he felt was flaming up in the same way in his own soul.

At ten o'clock the infantry that had been among the bushes in front of the battery and along the Kámenka streamlet retreated. From the battery they could be seen running back past it carrying their wounded on their muskets. A general with his suite came to the battery, and after speaking to the colonel gave Pierre an angry look and went away again having ordered the infantry supports behind the battery to lie down, so as to be less exposed to fire. After this from amid the ranks of infantry to the right of the battery came the sound of a drum and shouts of command, and from the battery one saw how those ranks of infantry moved forward.

Pierre looked over the wall of the trench and was particularly struck by a pale young officer who, letting his sword hang down, was walking backwards and kept glancing uneasily around.

The ranks of the infantry disappeared amid the smoke but their long-drawn shout and rapid musketry firing could still be heard. A few minutes later crowds of wounded men and stretcher-bearers came back from that direction. Projectiles began to fall still more frequently in the battery. Several men were lying about who had not been removed. Around the cannon the men moved still more briskly and busily. No one any longer took notice of Pierre. Once or twice he was shouted at for being in the way. The senior officer moved with big, rapid strides from one gun to another with a frowning face. The young officer, with his face still more flushed, commanded the men more scrupulously than ever. The soldiers handed up the charges, turned, loaded, and did their business with strained smartness. They gave little jumps as they walked, as though they were on springs.

The stormcloud had come upon them, and in every face the fire which Pierre had watched kindle burned up brightly. Pierre standing beside the commanding officer. The young officer, his hand to his shako, ran up to his superior.

"I have the honor to report, sir, that only eight rounds are left. Are we to continue firing?" he asked.

"Grapeshot!" the senior shouted, without answering the question, looking over the wall of the trench.

Suddenly something happened: the young officer gave a gasp and bending double sat down on the ground like a bird shot on the wing. Everything became strange, confused, and misty in Pierre's eyes.

One cannon ball after another whistled by and struck the earthwork, a soldier, or a gun. Pierre, who had not noticed these sounds before, now heard nothing else. On the right of the battery soldiers shouting "Hurrah!" were running not forwards but backwards, it seemed to Pierre.

A cannon ball struck the very end of the earth work by which he was standing, crumbling down the earth; a black ball flashed before his eyes and at the same instant plumped into something. Some militiamen who were entering the battery ran back.

"All with grapeshot!" shouted the officer.

The sergeant ran up to the officer and in a frightened whisper informed him (as a butler at dinner informs his master that there is no more of some wine asked for) that there were no more charges.

"The scoundrels! What are they doing?" shouted the officer, turning to Pierre.

The officer's face was red and perspiring and his eyes glittered under his frowning brow.

"Run to the reserves and bring up the ammunition boxes!" he yelled, angrily avoiding Pierre with his eyes and speaking to his men.

"I'll go," said Pierre.

The officer, without answering him, strode across to the opposite side.

"Don't fire.... Wait!" he shouted.

The man who had been ordered to go for ammunition stumbled against Pierre.

"Eh, sir, this is no place for you," said he, and ran down the slope.

Pierre ran after him, avoiding the spot where the young officer was sitting.

One cannon ball, another, and a third flew over him, falling in front, beside, and behind him. Pierre ran down the slope. "Where am I going?" he suddenly asked himself when he was already near the green ammunition wagons. He halted irresolutely, not knowing whether to return or go on. Suddenly a terrible concussion threw him backwards to the ground. At the same instant he was dazzled by a great flash of flame, and immediately a deafening roar, crackling, and whistling made his ears tingle.

When he came to himself he was sitting on the ground leaning on his hands; the ammunition wagons he had been approaching no longer existed, only charred green boards and rags littered the scorched grass, and a horse, dangling fragments of its shaft behind it, galloped past, while another horse lay, like Pierre, on the ground, uttering prolonged and piercing cries.

CHAPTER XXXII

B eside himself with terror Pierre jumped up and ran back to the battery, as to the only refuge from the horrors that surrounded him.

On entering the earthwork he noticed that there were men doing something there but that no shots were being fired from the battery. He had no time to realize who these men were. He saw the senior officer lying on the earth wall with his back turned as if he were examining something down below and that one of the soldiers he had noticed before was struggling forward shouting "Brothers!" and trying to free himself from some men who were holding him by the arm. He also saw something else that was strange.

But he had not time to realize that the colonel had been killed, that the soldier shouting "Brothers!" was a prisoner, and that another man had been bayoneted in the back before his eyes, for hardly had he run into the redoubt before a thin, sallow-faced, perspiring man in a blue uniform rushed on him sword in hand, shouting something. Instinctively guarding against the shock—for they had been running together at full speed before they saw one another—Pierre put out his hands and seized the man (a French officer) by the shoulder with one hand and by the throat with the other. The officer, dropping his sword, seized Pierre by his collar.

For some seconds they gazed with frightened eyes at one another's unfamiliar faces and both were perplexed at what they had done and what they were to do next. "Am I taken prisoner or have I taken him prisoner?" each was thinking. But the French officer was evidently more inclined to think he had been taken prisoner because Pierre's strong hand, impelled by instinctive fear, squeezed his throat ever tighter and tighter. The Frenchman was about to say something, when just above their heads, terrible and low, a cannon ball whistled, and it seemed to Pierre that the French officer's head had been torn off, so swiftly had he ducked it.

Pierre too bent his head and let his hands fall. Without further thought as to who had taken whom prisoner, the Frenchman ran back to the battery and Pierre ran down the slope stumbling over the dead and wounded who, it seemed to him, caught at his feet. But before he reached the foot of the knoll he was met by a dense crowd of Russian soldiers who, stumbling, tripping up, and shouting, ran merrily and wildly toward the battery. (This was the attack for which Ermólov claimed the credit, declaring that only his courage and good luck made such a feat possible: it was the attack in which he was said to have thrown some St. George's Crosses he had in his pocket into the battery for the first soldiers to take who got there.)

The French who had occupied the battery fled, and our troops shouting "Hurrah!" pursued them so far beyond the battery that it was difficult to call them back.

The prisoners were brought down from the battery and among them was a wounded French general, whom the officers surrounded. Crowds of wounded—some known to Pierre and some unknown— Russians and French, with faces distorted by suffering, walked, crawled, and were carried on stretchers from the battery. Pierre again went up onto the knoll where he had spent over an hour, and of that family circle which had received him as a member he did not find a single one. There were many dead whom he did not know, but some he recognized. The young officer still sat in the same way, bent double, in a pool of blood at the edge of the earth wall. The red-faced man was still twitching, but they did not carry him away.

Pierre ran down the slope once more.

"Now they will stop it, now they will be horrified at what they have done!" he thought, aimlessly going toward a crowd of stretcher bearers moving from the battlefield.

But behind the veil of smoke the sun was still high, and in front and especially to the left, near Semënovsk, something seemed to be seething in the smoke, and the roar of cannon and musketry did not diminish, but even increased to desperation like a man who, straining himself, shrieks with all his remaining strength.

CHAPTER XXXIII

The chief action of the battle of Borodinó was fought within the seven thousand feet between Borodinó and Bagratión's *flèches*. Beyond that space there was, on the one side, a demonstration made by the Russians with Uvárov's cavalry at midday, and on the other side, beyond Utítsa, Poniatowski's collision with Túchkov; but these two were detached and feeble actions in comparison with what took place in the center of the battlefield. On the field between Borodinó and the *flèches*, beside the wood, the chief action of the day took place on an open space visible from both sides and was fought in the simplest and most artless way.

The battle began on both sides with a cannonade from several hundred guns.

Then when the whole field was covered with smoke, two divisions, Campan's and Dessaix's, advanced from the French right, while Murat's troops advanced on Borodinó from their left.

From the Shevárdino Redoubt where Napoleon was standing the *flèches* were two thirds of a mile away, and it was more than a mile as the crow flies to Borodinó, so that Napoleon could not see what was happening there, especially as the smoke mingling with the mist hid the whole locality. The soldiers of Dessaix's division advancing against the *flèches* could only be seen till they had entered the hollow that lay between them and the *flèches*. As soon as they had descended into that hollow, the smoke of the guns and musketry on the *flèches* grew so dense that it covered the whole approach on that side of it. Through the smoke glimpses could be caught of something black—probably men—and at times the glint of bayonets. But whether they were moving or stationary, whether they were French or Russian, could not be discovered from the Shevárdino Redoubt.

The sun had risen brightly and its slanting rays struck straight into Napoleon's face as, shading his eyes with his hand, he looked at the *flèches*. The smoke spread out before them, and at times it looked as if the smoke were moving, at times as if the troops moved. Sometimes shouts were heard through the firing, but it was impossible to tell what was being done there.

Napoleon, standing on the knoll, looked through a field glass, and in its small circlet saw smoke and men, sometimes his own and sometimes Russians, but when he looked again with the naked eye, he could not tell where what he had seen was.

He descended the knoll and began walking up and down before it.

Occasionally he stopped, listened to the firing, and gazed intently at the battlefield.

But not only was it impossible to make out what was happening from where he was standing down below, or from the knoll above on which some of his generals had taken their stand, but even from the *flèches* themselves—in which by this time there were now Russian and now French soldiers, alternately or together, dead, wounded, alive, frightened, or maddened—even at those *flèches* themselves it was impossible to make out what was taking place. There for several hours amid incessant cannon and musketry fire, now Russians were seen alone, now Frenchmen alone, now infantry, and now cavalry: they appeared, fired, fell, collided, not knowing what to do with one another, screamed, and ran back again.

From the battlefield adjutants he had sent out, and orderlies from his marshals, kept galloping up to Napoleon with reports of the progress of the action, but all these reports were false, both because it was impossible in the heat of battle to say what was happening at any given moment and because many of the adjutants did not go to the actual place of conflict but reported what they had heard from others; and also because while an adjutant was riding more than a mile to Napoleon circumstances changed and the news he brought was already becoming false. Thus an adjutant galloped up from Murat with tidings that Borodinó had been occupied and the bridge over the

Kolochá was in the hands of the French. The adjutant asked whether Napoleon wished the troops to cross it? Napoleon gave orders that the troops should form up on the farther side and wait. But before that order was given—almost as soon in fact as the adjutant had left Borodinó—the bridge had been retaken by the Russians and burned, in the very skirmish at which Pierre had been present at the beginning of the battle.

An adjutant galloped up from the *flèches* with a pale and frightened face and reported to Napoleon that their attack had been repulsed, Campan wounded, and Davout killed; yet at the very time the adjutant had been told that the French had been repulsed, the *flèches* had in fact been recaptured by other French troops, and Davout was alive and only slightly bruised. On the basis of these necessarily untrustworthy reports Napoleon gave his orders, which had either been executed before he gave them or could not be and were not executed.

The marshals and generals, who were nearer to the field of battle but, like Napoleon, did not take part in the actual fighting and only occasionally went within musket range, made their own arrangements without asking Napoleon and issued orders where and in what direction to fire and where cavalry should gallop and infantry should run. But even their orders, like Napoleon's, were seldom carried out, and then but partially. For the most part things happened contrary to their orders. Soldiers ordered to advance ran back on meeting grapeshot; soldiers ordered to remain where they were, suddenly, seeing Russians unexpectedly before them, sometimes rushed back and sometimes forward, and the cavalry dashed without orders in pursuit of the flying Russians. In this way two cavalry regiments galloped through the Semënovsk hollow and as soon as they reached the top of the incline turned round and galloped full speed back again. The infantry moved in the same way, sometimes running to quite other places than those they were ordered to go to. All orders as to where and when to move the guns, when to send infantry to shoot or horsemen to ride down the Russian infantry— all such orders were given by the officers on the spot nearest to the units concerned, without asking either Ney, Davout, or Murat, much less Napoleon. They did not fear getting into trouble for not fulfilling orders or for acting on their own initiative, for in battle what is at stake is what is dearest to man—his own life—and it sometimes seems that safety lies in running back, sometimes in running forward; and these men who were right in the heat of the battle acted according to the mood of the moment. In reality, however, all these movements forward and backward did not improve or alter the position of the troops. All their rushing and galloping at one another did little harm, the harm of disablement and death was caused by the balls and bullets that flew over the fields on which these men were floundering about. As soon as they left the place where the balls and bullets were flying about, their superiors, located in the background, re-formed them and brought them under discipline and under the influence of that discipline led them back to the zone of fire, where under the influence of fear of death they lost their discipline and rushed about according to the chance promptings of the throng.

CHAPTER XXXIV

Napoleon's generals—Davout, Ney, and Murat, who were near that region of fire and sometimes even entered it—repeatedly led into it huge masses of well-ordered troops. But contrary to what had always happened in their former battles, instead of the news they expected of the enemy's flight, these orderly masses returned thence as disorganized and terrified mobs. The generals re-formed them, but their numbers constantly decreased. In the middle of the day Murat sent his adjutant to Napoleon to demand reinforcements.

Napoleon sat at the foot of the knoll, drinking punch, when Murat's adjutant galloped up with an assurance that the Russians would be routed if His Majesty would let him have another division.

"Reinforcements?" said Napoleon in a tone of stern surprise, looking at the adjutant—a handsome lad with long black curls arranged like Murat's own—as though he did not understand his words.

"Reinforcements!" thought Napoleon to himself. "How can they need reinforcements when they already have half the army directed against a weak, unentrenched Russian wing?"

"Tell the King of Naples," said he sternly, "that it is not noon yet, and I don't yet see my chessboard clearly. Go!..."

The handsome boy adjutant with the long hair sighed deeply without removing his hand from his hat and galloped back to where men were being slaughtered.

Napoleon rose and having summoned Caulaincourt and Berthier began talking to them about matters unconnected with the battle.

In the midst of this conversation, which was beginning to interest Napoleon, Berthier's eyes turned to look at a general with a suite, who was galloping toward the knoll on a lathering horse. It was Belliard. Having dismounted he went up to the Emperor with rapid strides and in a loud voice began boldly demonstrating the necessity of sending reinforcements. He swore on his honor that the Russians were lost if the Emperor would give another division.

Napoleon shrugged his shoulders and continued to pace up and down without replying. Belliard began talking loudly and eagerly to the generals of the suite around him.

"You are very fiery, Belliard," said Napoleon, when he again came up to the general. "In the heat of a battle it is easy to make a mistake. Go and have another look and then come back to me."

Before Belliard was out of sight, a messenger from another part of the battlefield galloped up.

"Now then, what do you want?" asked Napoleon in the tone of a man irritated at being continually disturbed.

"Sire, the prince..." began the adjutant.

"Asks for reinforcements?" said Napoleon with an angry gesture.

The adjutant bent his head affirmatively and began to report, but the Emperor turned from him, took a couple of steps, stopped, came back, and called Berthier.

"We must give reserves," he said, moving his arms slightly apart. "Who do you think should be sent there?" he asked of Berthier (whom he subsequently termed "that gosling I have made an eagle").

"Send Claparède's division, sire," replied Berthier, who knew all the division's regiments, and battalions by heart.

Napoleon nodded assent.

The adjutant galloped to Claparède's division and a few minutes later the Young Guards stationed behind the knoll moved forward. Napoleon gazed silently in that direction.

"No!" he suddenly said to Berthier. "I can't send Claparède. Send Friant's division."

Though there was no advantage in sending Friant's division instead of Claparède's, and even an obvious inconvenience and delay in stopping Claparède and sending Friant now, the order was carried out exactly. Napoleon did not notice that in regard to his army he was playing the part of a doctor who hinders by his medicines—a role he so justly understood and condemned.

Friant's division disappeared as the others had done into the smoke of the battlefield. From all sides adjutants continued to arrive at a gallop and as if by agreement all said the same thing. They all asked for reinforcements and all said that the Russians were holding their positions and maintaining a hellish fire under which the French army was melting away.

Napoleon sat on a campstool, wrapped in thought.

M. de Beausset, the man so fond of travel, having fasted since morning, came up to the Emperor and ventured respectfully to suggest lunch to His Majesty.

"I hope I may now congratulate Your Majesty on a victory?" said he.

Napoleon silently shook his head in negation. Assuming the negation to refer only to the victory and not to the lunch, M. de Beausset ventured with respectful jocularity to remark that there is no reason for not having lunch when one can get it.

"Go away..." exclaimed Napoleon suddenly and morosely, and turned aside.

A beatific smile of regret, repentance, and ecstasy beamed on M. de Beausset's face and he glided away to the other generals.

Napoleon was experiencing a feeling of depression like that of an ever-lucky gambler who, after recklessly flinging money about and always winning, suddenly just when he has calculated all the chances of the game, finds that the more he considers his play the more surely he loses.

His troops were the same, his generals the same, the same preparations had been made, the same dispositions, and the same proclamation *courte et énergique*, he himself was still the same: he knew that and knew that he was now even more experienced and skillful than before. Even the enemy was the same as at Austerlitz and Friedland—yet the terrible stroke of his arm had supernaturally become impotent.

All the old methods that had been unfailingly crowned with success: the concentration of batteries on one point, an attack by reserves to break the enemy's line, and a cavalry attack by "the men of iron," all these methods had already been employed, yet not only was there no victory, but from all sides came the same news of generals killed and wounded, of reinforcements needed, of the impossibility of driving back the Russians, and of disorganization among his own troops.

Formerly, after he had given two or three orders and uttered a few phrases, marshals and adjutants had come galloping up with congratulations and happy faces, announcing the trophies taken, the corps of prisoners, bundles of enemy eagles and standards, cannon and stores, and Murat had only begged leave to loose the cavalry to gather in the baggage wagons. So it had been at Lodi, Marengo, Arcola, Jena, Austerlitz, Wagram, and so on. But now something strange was happening to his troops.

Despite news of the capture of the *flèches*, Napoleon saw that this was not the same, not at all the same, as what had happened in his former battles. He saw that what he was feeling was felt by all the men about him experienced in the art of war. All their faces looked dejected, and they all shunned one another's eyes—only a de Beausset could fail to grasp the meaning of what was happening.

But Napoleon with his long experience of war well knew the meaning of a battle not gained by the attacking side in eight hours, after all efforts had been expended. He knew that it was a lost battle and that the least accident might now—with the fight balanced on such a strained center—destroy him and his army.

When he ran his mind over the whole of this strange Russian campaign in which not one battle had been won, and in which not a flag, or cannon, or army corps had been captured in two months, when he looked at the concealed depression on the faces around him and heard reports of the Russians still holding their ground—a terrible feeling like a nightmare took possession of him, and all the unlucky accidents that might destroy him occurred to his mind. The Russians might fall on his left wing, might break through his center, he himself might be killed by a stray cannon ball. All this was possible. In former battles he had only considered the possibilities of success, but now innumerable unlucky chances presented themselves, and he expected them all. Yes, it was like a dream in which a man fancies that a ruffian is coming to attack him, and raises his arm to strike that ruffian a terrible blow which he knows should annihilate him, but then feels that his arm drops powerless and limp like a rag, and the horror of unavoidable destruction seizes him in his helplessness.

The news that the Russians were attacking the left flank of the French army aroused that horror in Napoleon. He sat silently on a campstool below the knoll, with head bowed and elbows on his knees. Berthier approached and suggested that they should ride along the line to ascertain the position of affairs.

"What? What do you say?" asked Napoleon. "Yes, tell them to bring me my horse."

He mounted and rode toward Semënovsk.

Amid the powder smoke, slowly dispersing over the whole space through which Napoleon rode, horses and men were lying in pools of blood, singly or in heaps. Neither Napoleon nor any of his generals had ever before seen such horrors or so many slain in such a small area. The roar of guns, that had not ceased for ten hours, wearied the ear and gave a peculiar significance to the spectacle, as music does to *tableaux vivants*. Napoleon rode up the high ground at Semënovsk, and through the smoke saw ranks of men in uniforms of a color unfamiliar to him. They were Russians.

The Russians stood in serried ranks behind Semënovsk village and its knoll, and their guns boomed incessantly along their line and sent forth clouds of smoke. It was no longer a battle: it was a continuous slaughter which could be of no avail either to the French or the Russians. Napoleon stopped his horse and again fell into the reverie from which Berthier had aroused him. He could not stop what was going on before him and around him and was supposed to be directed by him and to depend on him, and from its lack of success this affair, for the first time, seemed to him unnecessary and horrible.

One of the generals rode up to Napoleon and ventured to offer to lead the Old Guard into action. Ney and Berthier, standing near Napoleon, exchanged looks and smiled contemptuously at this general's senseless offer.

Napoleon bowed his head and remained silent a long time.

"At eight hundred leagues from France, I will not have my Guard destroyed!" he said, and turning his horse rode back to Shevárdino.

CHAPTER XXXV

O n the rug-covered bench where Pierre had seen him in the
morning sat Kutúzov, his gray head hanging, his heavy body
relaxed. He gave no orders, but only assented to or dissented from
what others suggested.

"Yes, yes, do that," he replied to various proposals. "Yes, yes: go,
dear boy, and have a look," he would say to one or another of those
about him; or, "No, don't, we'd better wait!" He listened to the reports
that were brought him and gave directions when his subordinates
demanded that of him; but when listening to the reports it seemed
as if he were not interested in the import of the words spoken, but
rather in something else—in the expression of face and tone of voice
of those who were reporting. By long years of military experience he
knew, and with the wisdom of age understood, that it is impossible
for one man to direct hundreds of thousands of others struggling with
death, and he knew that the result of a battle is decided not by the
orders of a commander in chief, nor the place where the troops are
stationed, nor by the number of cannon or of slaughtered men, but by
that intangible force called the spirit of the army, and he watched this
force and guided it in as far as that was in his power.

Kutúzov's general expression was one of concentrated quiet
attention, and his face wore a strained look as if he found it difficult
to master the fatigue of his old and feeble body.

At eleven o'clock they brought him news that the *flèches* captured
by the French had been retaken, but that Prince Bagratión was
wounded. Kutúzov groaned and swayed his head.

"Ride over to Prince Peter Ivánovich and find out about it exactly," he said to one of his adjutants, and then turned to the Duke of Württemberg who was standing behind him.

"Will Your Highness please take command of the first army?"

Soon after the duke's departure—before he could possibly have reached Semënovsk—his adjutant came back from him and told Kutúzov that the duke asked for more troops.

Kutúzov made a grimace and sent an order to Dokhtúrov to take over the command of the first army, and a request to the duke—whom he said he could not spare at such an important moment—to return to him. When they brought him news that Murat had been taken prisoner, and the staff officers congratulated him, Kutúzov smiled.

"Wait a little, gentlemen," said he. "The battle is won, and there is nothing extraordinary in the capture of Murat. Still, it is better to wait before we rejoice."

But he sent an adjutant to take the news round the army.

When Scherbínin came galloping from the left flank with news that the French had captured the *flèches* and the village of Semënovsk, Kutúzov, guessing by the sounds of the battle and by Scherbínin's looks that the news was bad, rose as if to stretch his legs and, taking Scherbínin's arm, led him aside.

"Go, my dear fellow," he said to Ermólov, "and see whether something can't be done."

Kutúzov was in Górki, near the center of the Russian position. The attack directed by Napoleon against our left flank had been several times repulsed. In the center the French had not got beyond Borodinó, and on their left flank Uvárov's cavalry had put the French to flight.

Toward three o'clock the French attacks ceased. On the faces of all who came from the field of battle, and of those who stood around him, Kutúzov noticed an expression of extreme tension. He was satisfied with the day's success—a success exceeding his expectations, but the old man's strength was failing him. Several times his head dropped low as if it were falling and he dozed off. Dinner was brought him.

Adjutant General Wolzogen, the man who when riding past Prince Andrew had said, "the war should be extended widely," and whom Bagratión so detested, rode up while Kutúzov was at dinner. Wolzogen had come from Barclay de Tolly to report on the progress of affairs on the left flank. The sagacious Barclay de Tolly, seeing crowds of wounded men running back and the disordered rear of the army, weighed all the circumstances, concluded that the battle was lost, and sent his favorite officer to the commander in chief with that news.

Kutúzov was chewing a piece of roast chicken with difficulty and glanced at Wolzogen with eyes that brightened under their puckering lids.

Wolzogen, nonchalantly stretching his legs, approached Kutúzov with a half-contemptuous smile on his lips, scarcely touching the peak of his cap.

He treated his Serene Highness with a somewhat affected nonchalance intended to show that, as a highly trained military man, he left it to Russians to make an idol of this useless old man, but that he knew whom he was dealing with. *"Der alte Herr"* (as in their own set the Germans called Kutúzov) "is making himself very comfortable," thought Wolzogen, and looking severely at the dishes in front of Kutúzov he began to report to "the old gentleman" the position of affairs on the left flank as Barclay had ordered him to and as he himself had seen and understood it.

"All the points of our position are in the enemy's hands and we cannot dislodge them for lack of troops, the men are running away and it is impossible to stop them," he reported.

Kutúzov ceased chewing and fixed an astonished gaze on Wolzogen, as if not understanding what was said to him. Wolzogen, noticing "the old gentleman's" agitation, said with a smile:

"I have not considered it right to conceal from your Serene Highness what I have seen. The troops are in complete disorder...."

"You have seen? You have seen?..." Kutúzov shouted. Frowning and rising quickly, he went up to Wolzogen.

"How... how dare you!..." he shouted, choking and making a threatening gesture with his trembling arms: "How dare you, sir, say that to *me?* You know nothing about it. Tell General Barclay from me that his information is incorrect and that the real course of the battle is better known to me, the commander in chief, than to him."

Wolzogen was about to make a rejoinder, but Kutúzov interrupted him.

"The enemy has been repulsed on the left and defeated on the right flank. If you have seen amiss, sir, do not allow yourself to say what you don't know! Be so good as to ride to General Barclay and inform him of my firm intention to attack the enemy tomorrow," said Kutúzov sternly.

All were silent, and the only sound audible was the heavy breathing of the panting old general.

"They are repulsed everywhere, for which I thank God and our brave army! The enemy is beaten, and tomorrow we shall drive him from the sacred soil of Russia," said Kutúzov crossing himself, and he suddenly sobbed as his eyes filled with tears.

Wolzogen, shrugging his shoulders and curling his lips, stepped silently aside, marveling at "the old gentleman's" conceited stupidity.

"Ah, here he is, my hero!" said Kutúzov to a portly, handsome, dark-haired general who was just ascending the knoll.

This was Raévski, who had spent the whole day at the most important part of the field of Borodinó.

Raévski reported that the troops were firmly holding their ground and that the French no longer ventured to attack.

After hearing him, Kutúzov said in French:

"Then you do not think, *like some others*, that we must retreat?"

"On the contrary, your Highness, in indecisive actions it is always the most stubborn who remain victors," replied Raévski, "and in my opinion..."

"Kaysárov!" Kutúzov called to his adjutant. "Sit down and write out the order of the day for tomorrow. And you," he continued, addressing another, "ride along the line and announce that tomorrow we attack."

While Kutúzov was talking to Raévski and dictating the order of the day, Wolzogen returned from Barclay and said that General Barclay wished to have written confirmation of the order the field marshal had given.

Kutúzov, without looking at Wolzogen, gave directions for the order to be written out which the former commander in chief, to avoid personal responsibility, very judiciously wished to receive.

And by means of that mysterious indefinable bond which maintains throughout an army one and the same temper, known as "the spirit of the army," and which constitutes the sinew of war, Kutúzov's words, his order for a battle next day, immediately became known from one end of the army to the other.

It was far from being the same words or the same order that reached the farthest links of that chain. The tales passing from mouth to mouth at different ends of the army did not even resemble what Kutúzov had said, but the sense of his words spread everywhere because what he said was not the outcome of cunning calculations, but of a feeling that lay in the commander in chief's soul as in that of every Russian.

And on learning that tomorrow they were to attack the enemy, and hearing from the highest quarters a confirmation of what they wanted to believe, the exhausted, wavering men felt comforted and inspirited.

CHAPTER XXXVI

Prince Andrew's regiment was among the reserves which till after one o'clock were stationed inactive behind Semënovsk, under heavy artillery fire. Toward two o'clock the regiment, having already lost more than two hundred men, was moved forward into a trampled oatfield in the gap between Semënovsk and the Knoll Battery, where thousands of men perished that day and on which an intense, concentrated fire from several hundred enemy guns was directed between one and two o'clock.

Without moving from that spot or firing a single shot the regiment here lost another third of its men. From in front and especially from the right, in the unlifting smoke the guns boomed, and out of the mysterious domain of smoke that overlay the whole space in front, quick hissing cannon balls and slow whistling shells flew unceasingly. At times, as if to allow them a respite, a quarter of an hour passed during which the cannon balls and shells all flew overhead, but sometimes several men were torn from the regiment in a minute and the slain were continually being dragged away and the wounded carried off.

With each fresh blow less and less chance of life remained for those not yet killed. The regiment stood in columns of battalion, three hundred paces apart, but nevertheless the men were always in one and the same mood. All alike were taciturn and morose. Talk was rarely heard in the ranks, and it ceased altogether every time the thud of a successful shot and the cry of "stretchers!" was heard. Most of the time, by their officers' order, the men sat on the ground. One, having taken off his shako, carefully loosened the gathers of its lining and drew them tight again; another, rubbing some dry clay between his palms, polished his bayonet; another fingered the strap and pulled the buckle of his bandolier, while another smoothed and refolded his leg bands and put his boots on again. Some built little houses of the tufts in the plowed ground, or plaited baskets from the straw in the cornfield. All seemed fully absorbed in these pursuits. When men were killed or wounded, when rows of stretchers went past, when some troops retreated, and when great masses of the enemy came into view through the smoke, no one paid any attention to these things. But when our artillery or cavalry advanced or some of our infantry were seen to move forward, words of approval were heard on all sides. But the liveliest attention was attracted by occurrences quite apart from, and unconnected with, the battle. It was as if the minds of these morally exhausted men found relief in everyday, commonplace occurrences. A battery of artillery was passing in front of the regiment. The horse of an ammunition cart put its leg over a trace. "Hey, look at the trace horse!... Get her leg out! She'll fall.... Ah, they don't see it!" came identical shouts from the ranks all along the regiment. Another time, general attention was attracted by a small brown dog, coming heaven knows whence, which trotted in a preoccupied manner in front of the ranks with tail stiffly erect till suddenly a shell fell close by, when it yelped, tucked its tail between its legs, and darted aside. Yells and shrieks of laughter rose from the whole regiment. But such distractions lasted only a moment, and for eight hours the men had been inactive, without food, in constant fear of death, and their pale and gloomy faces grew ever paler and gloomier.

Prince Andrew, pale and gloomy like everyone in the regiment, paced up and down from the border of one patch to another, at the edge of the meadow beside an oatfield, with head bowed and arms behind his back. There was nothing for him to do and no orders to be given. Everything went on of itself. The killed were dragged from the front, the wounded carried away, and the ranks closed up. If any soldiers ran to the rear they returned immediately and hastily. At first Prince Andrew, considering it his duty to rouse the courage of the men and to set them an example, walked about among the ranks, but he soon became convinced that this was unnecessary and that there was nothing he could teach them. All the powers of his soul, as of every soldier there, were unconsciously bent on avoiding the contemplation of the horrors of their situation. He walked along the meadow, dragging his feet, rustling the grass, and gazing at the dust that covered his boots; now he took big strides trying to keep to the footprints left on the meadow by the mowers, then he counted his steps, calculating how often he must walk from one strip to another to walk a mile, then he stripped the flowers from the wormwood that grew along a boundary rut, rubbed them in his palms, and smelled their pungent, sweetly bitter scent. Nothing remained of the previous day's thoughts. He thought of nothing. He listened with weary ears to the ever-recurring sounds, distinguishing the whistle of flying projectiles from the booming of the reports, glanced at the tiresomely familiar faces of the men of the first battalion, and waited. "Here it comes... this one is coming our way again!" he thought, listening to an approaching whistle in the hidden region of smoke. "One, another! Again! It has hit...." He stopped and looked at the ranks. "No, it has gone over. But this one has hit!" And again he started trying to reach the boundary strip in sixteen paces. A whizz and a thud! Five paces from him, a cannon ball tore up the dry earth and disappeared. A chill ran down his back. Again he glanced at the ranks. Probably many had been hit—a large crowd had gathered near the second battalion.

"Adjutant!" he shouted. "Order them not to crowd together."

The adjutant, having obeyed this instruction, approached Prince Andrew. From the other side a battalion commander rode up.

"Look out!" came a frightened cry from a soldier and, like a bird whirring in rapid flight and alighting on the ground, a shell dropped with little noise within two steps of Prince Andrew and close to the battalion commander's horse. The horse first, regardless of whether it was right or wrong to show fear, snorted, reared almost throwing the major, and galloped aside. The horse's terror infected the men.

"Lie down!" cried the adjutant, throwing himself flat on the ground.

Prince Andrew hesitated. The smoking shell spun like a top between him and the prostrate adjutant, near a wormwood plant between the field and the meadow.

"Can this be death?" thought Prince Andrew, looking with a quite new, envious glance at the grass, the wormwood, and the streamlet of smoke that curled up from the rotating black ball. "I cannot, I do not wish to die. I love life—I love this grass, this earth, this air...." He thought this, and at the same time remembered that people were looking at him.

"It's shameful, sir!" he said to the adjutant. "What..."

He did not finish speaking. At one and the same moment came the sound of an explosion, a whistle of splinters as from a breaking window frame, a suffocating smell of powder, and Prince Andrew started to one side, raising his arm, and fell on his chest. Several officers ran up to him. From the right side of his abdomen, blood was welling out making a large stain on the grass.

The militiamen with stretchers who were called up stood behind the officers. Prince Andrew lay on his chest with his face in the grass, breathing heavily and noisily.

"What are you waiting for? Come along!"

The peasants went up and took him by his shoulders and legs, but he moaned piteously and, exchanging looks, they set him down again.

"Pick him up, lift him, it's all the same!" cried someone.

They again took him by the shoulders and laid him on the stretcher.

"Ah, God! My God! What is it? The stomach? That means death! My God!"—voices among the officers were heard saying.

"It flew a hair's breadth past my ear," said the adjutant.

The peasants, adjusting the stretcher to their shoulders, started hurriedly along the path they had trodden down, to the dressing station.

"Keep in step! Ah... those peasants!" shouted an officer, seizing by their shoulders and checking the peasants, who were walking unevenly and jolting the stretcher.

"Get into step, Fëdor... I say, Fëdor!" said the foremost peasant.

"Now that's right!" said the one behind joyfully, when he had got into step.

"Your excellency! Eh, Prince!" said the trembling voice of Timókhin, who had run up and was looking down on the stretcher.

Prince Andrew opened his eyes and looked up at the speaker from the stretcher into which his head had sunk deep and again his eyelids drooped.

The militiamen carried Prince Andrew to the dressing station by the wood, where wagons were stationed. The dressing station consisted of three tents with flaps turned back, pitched at the edge of a birch wood. In the wood, wagons and horses were standing. The horses were eating oats from their movable troughs and sparrows flew down and pecked the grains that fell. Some crows, scenting blood, flew among the birch trees cawing impatiently. Around the tents, over more than five acres, bloodstained men in various garbs stood, sat, or lay. Around the wounded stood crowds of soldier stretcher-bearers with dismal and attentive faces, whom the officers keeping order tried in vain to drive from the spot. Disregarding the officers' orders, the soldiers stood leaning against their stretchers and gazing intently, as if trying to comprehend the difficult problem of what was taking place before them. From the tents came now loud angry cries and now plaintive groans. Occasionally dressers ran out to fetch water, or to point out those who were to be brought in next. The wounded men awaiting their turn outside the tents groaned, sighed, wept, screamed, swore, or asked for vodka. Some were delirious. Prince Andrew's bearers, stepping over the wounded who had not yet been bandaged, took him, as a regimental commander, close up to one of the tents and there stopped, awaiting instructions. Prince Andrew opened his eyes and for a long time could not make out what was going on around him. He remembered the meadow, the wormwood, the field, the whirling black ball, and his sudden rush of passionate love of life. Two steps from him, leaning against a branch and talking loudly and attracting general attention, stood a tall, handsome, black-haired noncommissioned officer with a bandaged head. He had been wounded in the head and leg by bullets. Around him, eagerly listening to his talk, a crowd of wounded and stretcher-bearers was gathered.

"We kicked *him* out from there so that he chucked everything, we grabbed the King himself!" cried he, looking around him with eyes that glittered with fever. "If only reserves had come up just then, lads, there wouldn't have been nothing left of him! I tell you surely...."

Like all the others near the speaker, Prince Andrew looked at him with shining eyes and experienced a sense of comfort. "But isn't it all the same now?" thought he. "And what will be there, and what has there been here? Why was I so reluctant to part with life? There was something in this life I did not and do not understand."

CHAPTER XXXVII

O ne of the doctors came out of the tent in a bloodstained apron, holding a cigar between the thumb and little finger of one of his small bloodstained hands, so as not to smear it. He raised his head and looked about him, but above the level of the wounded men. He evidently wanted a little respite. After turning his head from right to left for some time, he sighed and looked down.

"All right, immediately," he replied to a dresser who pointed Prince Andrew out to him, and he told them to carry him into the tent.

Murmurs arose among the wounded who were waiting.

"It seems that even in the next world only the gentry are to have a chance!" remarked one.

Prince Andrew was carried in and laid on a table that had only just been cleared and which a dresser was washing down. Prince Andrew could not make out distinctly what was in that tent. The pitiful groans from all sides and the torturing pain in his thigh, stomach, and back distracted him. All he saw about him merged into a general impression of naked, bleeding human bodies that seemed to fill the whole of the low tent, as a few weeks previously, on that hot August day, such bodies had filled the dirty pond beside the Smolénsk road. Yes, it was the same flesh, the same *chair à canon*, the sight of which had even then filled him with horror, as by a presentiment.

There were three operating tables in the tent. Two were occupied, and on the third they placed Prince Andrew. For a little while he was left alone and involuntarily witnessed what was taking place on the other two tables. On the nearest one sat a Tartar, probably a Cossack, judging by the uniform thrown down beside him. Four soldiers were holding him, and a spectacled doctor was cutting into his muscular brown back.

"Ooh, ooh, ooh!" grunted the Tartar, and suddenly lifting up his swarthy snub-nosed face with its high cheekbones, and baring his white teeth, he began to wriggle and twitch his body and utter piercing, ringing, and prolonged yells. On the other table, round which many people were crowding, a tall well-fed man lay on his back with his head thrown back. His curly hair, its color, and the shape of his head seemed strangely familiar to Prince Andrew. Several dressers were pressing on his chest to hold him down. One large, white, plump leg twitched rapidly all the time with a feverish tremor. The man was sobbing and choking convulsively. Two doctors—one of whom was pale and trembling—were silently doing something to this man's other, gory leg. When he had finished with the Tartar, whom they covered with an overcoat, the spectacled doctor came up to Prince Andrew, wiping his hands.

He glanced at Prince Andrew's face and quickly turned away.

"Undress him! What are you waiting for?" he cried angrily to the dressers.

His very first, remotest recollections of childhood came back to Prince Andrew's mind when the dresser with sleeves rolled up began hastily to undo the buttons of his clothes and undressed him. The doctor bent down over the wound, felt it, and sighed deeply. Then he made a sign to someone, and the torturing pain in his abdomen caused Prince Andrew to lose consciousness. When he came to himself the splintered portions of his thighbone had been extracted, the torn flesh cut away, and the wound bandaged. Water was being sprinkled on his face. As soon as Prince Andrew opened his eyes, the doctor bent over, kissed him silently on the lips, and hurried away.

After the sufferings he had been enduring, Prince Andrew enjoyed a blissful feeling such as he had not experienced for a long time. All the best and happiest moments of his life—especially his earliest childhood, when he used to be undressed and put to bed, and when leaning over him his nurse sang him to sleep and he, burying his head in the pillow, felt happy in the mere consciousness of life—returned to his memory, not merely as something past but as something present.

The doctors were busily engaged with the wounded man the shape of whose head seemed familiar to Prince Andrew: they were lifting him up and trying to quiet him.

"Show it to me.... Oh, ooh... Oh! Oh, ooh!" his frightened moans could be heard, subdued by suffering and broken by sobs.

Hearing those moans Prince Andrew wanted to weep. Whether because he was dying without glory, or because he was sorry to part with life, or because of those memories of a childhood that could not return, or because he was suffering and others were suffering and that man near him was groaning so piteously—he felt like weeping childlike, kindly, and almost happy tears.

The wounded man was shown his amputated leg stained with clotted blood and with the boot still on.

"Oh! Oh, ooh!" he sobbed, like a woman.

The doctor who had been standing beside him, preventing Prince Andrew from seeing his face, moved away.

"My God! What is this? Why is he here?" said Prince Andrew to himself.

In the miserable, sobbing, enfeebled man whose leg had just been amputated, he recognized Anatole Kurágin. Men were supporting him in their arms and offering him a glass of water, but his trembling, swollen lips could not grasp its rim. Anatole was sobbing painfully. "Yes, it is he! Yes, that man is somehow closely and painfully connected with me," thought Prince Andrew, not yet clearly grasping what he saw before him. "What is the connection of that man with my childhood and life?" he asked himself without finding an answer. And suddenly a new unexpected memory from that realm of pure and loving childhood presented itself to him. He remembered Natásha as he had seen her for the first time at the ball in 1810, with her slender neck and arms and with a frightened happy face ready for rapture, and love and tenderness for her, stronger and more vivid than ever, awoke in his soul. He now remembered the connection that existed between himself and this man who was dimly gazing at him through tears that filled his swollen eyes. He remembered everything, and ecstatic pity and love for that man overflowed his happy heart.

Prince Andrew could no longer restrain himself and wept tender loving tears for his fellow men, for himself, and for his own and their errors.

"Compassion, love of our brothers, for those who love us and for those who hate us, love of our enemies; yes, that love which God preached on earth and which Princess Mary taught me and I did not understand—that is what made me sorry to part with life, that is what remained for me had I lived. But now it is too late. I know it!"

CHAPTER XXXVIII

The terrible spectacle of the battlefield covered with dead and wounded, together with the heaviness of his head and the news that some twenty generals he knew personally had been killed or wounded, and the consciousness of the impotence of his once mighty arm, produced an unexpected impression on Napoleon who usually liked to look at the killed and wounded, thereby, he considered, testing his strength of mind. This day the horrible appearance of the battlefield overcame that strength of mind which he thought constituted his merit and his greatness. He rode hurriedly from the battlefield and returned to the Shevárdino knoll, where he sat on his campstool, his sallow face swollen and heavy, his eyes dim, his nose red, and his voice hoarse, involuntarily listening, with downcast eyes, to the sounds of firing. With painful dejection he awaited the end of this action, in which he regarded himself as a participant and which he was unable to arrest. A personal, human feeling for a brief moment got the better of the artificial phantasm of life he had served so long. He felt in his own person the sufferings and death he had witnessed on the battlefield. The heaviness of his head and chest reminded him of the possibility of suffering and death for himself. At that moment he did not desire Moscow, or victory, or glory (what need had he for any more glory?). The one thing he wished for was rest, tranquillity, and freedom. But when he had been on the Semënovsk heights the artillery commander had proposed to him to bring several batteries of artillery up to those heights to strengthen the fire on the Russian troops crowded in front of Knyazkóvo. Napoleon had assented and had given orders that news should be brought to him of the effect those batteries produced.

An adjutant came now to inform him that the fire of two hundred guns had been concentrated on the Russians, as he had ordered, but that they still held their ground.

"Our fire is mowing them down by rows, but still they hold on," said the adjutant.

"They want more!..." said Napoleon in a hoarse voice.

"Sire?" asked the adjutant who had not heard the remark.

"They want more!" croaked Napoleon frowning. "Let them have it!"

Even before he gave that order the thing he did not desire, and for which he gave the order only because he thought it was expected of him, was being done. And he fell back into that artificial realm of imaginary greatness, and again—as a horse walking a treadmill thinks it is doing something for itself—he submissively fulfilled the cruel, sad, gloomy, and inhuman role predestined for him.

And not for that day and hour alone were the mind and conscience darkened of this man on whom the responsibility for what was happening lay more than on all the others who took part in it. Never to the end of his life could he understand goodness, beauty, or truth, or the significance of his actions which were too contrary to goodness and truth, too remote from everything human, for him ever to be able to grasp their meaning. He could not disavow his actions, belauded as they were by half the world, and so he had to repudiate truth, goodness, and all humanity.

Not only on that day, as he rode over the battlefield strewn with men killed and maimed (by his will as he believed), did he reckon as he looked at them how many Russians there were for each Frenchman and, deceiving himself, find reason for rejoicing in the calculation that there were five Russians for every Frenchman. Not on that day alone did he write in a letter to Paris that "the battle field was superb," because fifty thousand corpses lay there, but even on the island of St. Helena in the peaceful solitude where he said he intended to devote his leisure to an account of the great deeds he had done, he wrote:

The Russian war should have been the most popular war of modern times: it was a war of good sense, for real interests, for the tranquillity and security of all; it was purely pacific and conservative.

It was a war for a great cause, the end of uncertainties and the beginning of security. A new horizon and new labors were opening out, full of well-being and prosperity for all. The European system was already founded; all that remained was to organize it.

Satisfied on these great points and with tranquility everywhere, I too should have had my *Congress* and my *Holy Alliance*. Those ideas were stolen from me. In that reunion of great sovereigns we should have discussed our interests like one family, and have rendered account to the peoples as clerk to master.

Europe would in this way soon have been, in fact, but one people, and anyone who traveled anywhere would have found himself always in the common fatherland. I should have demanded the freedom of all navigable rivers for everybody, that the seas should be common to all, and that the great standing armies should be reduced henceforth to mere guards for the sovereigns.

On returning to France, to the bosom of the great, strong, magnificent, peaceful, and glorious fatherland, I should have proclaimed her frontiers immutable; all future wars purely *defensive*, all aggrandizement *antinational*. I should have associated my son in the Empire; my *dictatorship* would have been finished, and his constitutional reign would have begun.

Paris would have been the capital of the world, and the French the envy of the nations!

My leisure then, and my old age, would have been devoted, in company with the Empress and during the royal apprenticeship of my son, to leisurely visiting, with our own horses and like a true country couple, every corner of the Empire, receiving complaints, redressing wrongs, and scattering public buildings and benefactions on all sides and everywhere.

Napoleon, predestined by Providence for the gloomy role of executioner of the peoples, assured himself that the aim of his actions had been the peoples' welfare and that he could control the fate of millions and by the employment of power confer benefactions.

"Of four hundred thousand who crossed the Vistula," he wrote further of the Russian war, "half were Austrians, Prussians, Saxons, Poles, Bavarians, Württembergers, Mecklenburgers, Spaniards, Italians, and Neapolitans. The Imperial army, strictly speaking, was one third composed of Dutch, Belgians, men from the borders of the Rhine, Piedmontese, Swiss, Genevese, Tuscans, Romans, inhabitants of the Thirty-second Military Division, of Bremen, of Hamburg, and so on: it included scarcely a hundred and forty thousand who spoke French. The Russian expedition actually cost France less than fifty thousand men; the Russian army in its retreat from Vílna to Moscow lost in the various battles four times more men than the French army; the burning of Moscow cost the lives of a hundred thousand Russians who died of cold and want in the woods; finally, in its march from Moscow to the Oder the Russian army also suffered from the severity of the season; so that by the time it reached Vílna it numbered only fifty thousand, and at Kálisch less than eighteen thousand."

He imagined that the war with Russia came about by his will, and the horrors that occurred did not stagger his soul. He boldly took the whole responsibility for what happened, and his darkened mind found justification in the belief that among the hundreds of thousands who perished there were fewer Frenchmen than Hessians and Bavarians.

CHAPTER XXXIX

Several tens of thousands of the slain lay in diverse postures and various uniforms on the fields and meadows belonging to the Davýdov family and to the crown serfs—those fields and meadows where for hundreds of years the peasants of Borodinó, Górki, Shevárdino, and Seménovsk had reaped their harvests and pastured their cattle. At the dressing stations the grass and earth were soaked with blood for a space of some three acres around. Crowds of men of various arms, wounded and unwounded, with frightened faces, dragged themselves back to Mozháysk from the one army and back to Valúevo from the other. Other crowds, exhausted and hungry, went forward led by their officers. Others held their ground and continued to fire.

Over the whole field, previously so gaily beautiful with the glitter of bayonets and cloudlets of smoke in the morning sun, there now spread a mist of damp and smoke and a strange acid smell of saltpeter and blood. Clouds gathered and drops of rain began to fall on the dead and wounded, on the frightened, exhausted, and hesitating men, as if to say: "Enough, men! Enough! Cease... bethink yourselves! What are you doing?"

To the men of both sides alike, worn out by want of food and rest, it began equally to appear doubtful whether they should continue to slaughter one another; all the faces expressed hesitation, and the question arose in every soul: "For what, for whom, must I kill and be killed?... You may go and kill whom you please, but I don't want to do so any more!" By evening this thought had ripened in every soul. At any moment these men might have been seized with horror at what they were doing and might have thrown up everything and run away anywhere.

But though toward the end of the battle the men felt all the horror of what they were doing, though they would have been glad to leave off, some incomprehensible, mysterious power continued to control them, and they still brought up the charges, loaded, aimed, and applied the match, though only one artilleryman survived out of every three, and though they stumbled and panted with fatigue, perspiring and stained with blood and powder. The cannon balls flew just as swiftly and cruelly from both sides, crushing human bodies, and that terrible work which was not done by the will of a man but at the will of Him who governs men and worlds continued.

Anyone looking at the disorganized rear of the Russian army would have said that, if only the French made one more slight effort, it would disappear; and anyone looking at the rear of the French army would have said that the Russians need only make one more slight effort and the French would be destroyed. But neither the French nor the Russians made that effort, and the flame of battle burned slowly out.

The Russians did not make that effort because they were not attacking the French. At the beginning of the battle they stood blocking the way to Moscow and they still did so at the end of the battle as at the beginning. But even had the aim of the Russians been to drive the French from their positions, they could not have made this last effort, for all the Russian troops had been broken up, there was no part of the Russian army that had not suffered in the battle, and though still holding their positions they had lost ONE HALF of their army.

The French, with the memory of all their former victories during fifteen years, with the assurance of Napoleon's invincibility, with the consciousness that they had captured part of the battlefield and had lost only a quarter of their men and still had their Guards intact, twenty thousand strong, might easily have made that effort. The French who had attacked the Russian army in order to drive it from its position ought to have made that effort, for as long as the Russians continued to block the road to Moscow as before, the aim of the French had not been attained and all their efforts and losses were in vain. But the French did not make that effort. Some historians say that Napoleon need only have used his Old Guards, who were intact, and the battle would have been won. To speak of what would have happened had Napoleon sent his Guards is like talking of what would happen if autumn became spring. It could not be. Napoleon did not give his Guards, not because he did not want to, but because it could not be done. All the generals, officers, and soldiers of the French army knew it could not be done, because the flagging spirit of the troops would not permit it.

It was not Napoleon alone who had experienced that nightmare feeling of the mighty arm being stricken powerless, but all the generals and soldiers of his army whether they had taken part in the battle or not, after all their experience of previous battles—when after one tenth of such efforts the enemy had fled—experienced a similar feeling of terror before an enemy who, after losing HALF his men, stood as threateningly at the end as at the beginning of the battle. The moral force of the attacking French army was exhausted. Not that sort of victory which is defined by the capture of pieces of material fastened to sticks, called standards, and of the ground on which the troops had stood and were standing, but a moral victory that convinces the enemy of the moral superiority of his opponent and of his own impotence was gained by the Russians at Borodinó. The French invaders, like an infuriated animal that has in its onslaught received a mortal wound, felt that they were perishing, but could not stop, any more than the Russian army, weaker by one half, could help swerving. By impetus gained, the French army was still able to roll forward to Moscow, but there, without further effort on the part of the Russians, it had to perish, bleeding from the mortal wound it had received at Borodinó. The direct consequence of the battle of Borodinó was Napoleon's senseless flight from Moscow, his retreat along the old Smolénsk road, the destruction of the invading army of five hundred thousand men, and the downfall of Napoleonic France, on which at Borodinó for the first time the hand of an opponent of stronger spirit had been laid.